THE LOST SEA

TOBY J NICHOLS

SEVERED PRESS
HOBART TASMANIA

THE LOST SEA

Copyright © 2020 Toby J Nichols

WWW.SEVEREDPRESS.COM

ISBN: 978-1-922323-67-5

CHAPTER 1

Jessie Hall heard the chopper before he saw it. He slung his water container and cooler, filled with food, in the back of his R22 helicopter and waited for Rory to come into view. He squinted up at the gray dawn sky, waiting for the familiar speck, while willing away the spark that seeing his neighbor always brought.

Jessie, his stockman Baz, and neighbor Rory would be spending the next few weeks together, mustering Jessie's cattle then Rory's. While their farms were next to each other, they couldn't exactly pop 'round for beer—at least not by car. Which was probably a good thing. Because the times they did get together to socialize were hazardous. Jessie was never quite sure where he stood, or where he wanted to be standing around Rory.

The black dot became the chopper then it was landing, kicking up dust and making the air pulse. The blades slowed and spun to a lazy stop.

Rory took off his headphones and hopped out. "Hey, nice morning for it."

Rory, eternally happy, a regular Mr. Fucking Sunshine.

Jessie didn't allow himself a smile. He'd be friendly but keep his distance the same as usual, even though Rory made it tempting to cross that line. "Yeah."

"You had some flooding?"

"No?" That was a weird question.

Rory shrugged. "Thought I saw the glint of water inland. Thought it was weird."

"Yeah. Maybe you need to go and get your eyes checked."

Rory chuckled. The corner of his eyes crinkled. Jessie had to look away. This infatuation was ridiculous. Dangerous. He'd been able to keep it in check, then Amy had decided to leave. Too much distance...and she hadn't meant the cattle station but the acres between them. With her gone, it had been harder to avoid the sting of attraction.

He'd tried to make it work with her, to prove what kind of man he was. And he'd failed. Now he didn't know what to do.

Jessie whistled and his red heeler, Rosie, came tearing around from the side of the shed. He was pretty sure Rosie missed Amy more than he did. Rory squatted down and gave her a proper greeting, scratching under her ears and the scruff of her neck. Rosie licked his face and neck like they were best friends. She liked everyone more than him, even though she'd been his dog for close to ten years. Most of the time he didn't blame her. He didn't like himself either.

"Opal's going to drop a litter in a couple of weeks. You want one?"

No was the word that formed on his lips. He liked Rosie; she was a good dog. Did her job and aside from being overly friendly with Rory, he couldn't fault her. But she wasn't getting any younger. Nor was he. Forty was rushing toward him too fast. He glanced at Rosie; she could help teach a pup. He was only resisting because Rory was offering.

Get a grip. He nodded. "Maybe. Carton of bear?"

"Nah, it's on me, mate." Rory stood. "Rosie needs a buddy and a bit of help with the work."

"Is that what she was whispering in your ear?" He was not jealous of the easy affection.

Rory just grinned. Jessie almost smiled.

"Who are we waiting for?"

"My useless nephew and Baz."

Rory raised his eyebrows in question. They hadn't spoken in close to three months. Not that there was much gossip to

3

share. They both lived alone on their stations. Well, he had been alone until Mike needed a place to go.

"Mike got kicked out of school so my brother thought it would be a good idea for him to come here for the rest of the year. You know, so the station could knock some sense into him." It hadn't worked for Jessie and he was still waiting.

"You don't think it's helping?"

Jessie leveled his gaze at Rory. "He arrived with green hair and four piercings...he now has six and blue hair."

"What is he, seventeen? Eighteen?"

"A pain in the ass. He won't lift a finger outside or inside." Which was worse than useless. Mike was a hindrance. Always there, always in the way. He was no longer the kid who'd come out for holidays and gleefully attempted every job. Jessie hadn't recognized Mike when he'd picked him up. Two years without a visit and the kid was long gone, replaced by a teen, almost a man, who didn't want to participate in anything and wouldn't take a chance.

Jessie glanced at Rory and knew exactly where Mike got it from, and it wasn't from his dad. Taking a shot meant putting something on the line and Jessie had nothing he was willing to risk.

The silence between them was filled with bird chatter.

Finally, Rory spoke. "Have you tried talking to him? He used to come out here a lot, right?"

4

"Yes and yes. Same nephew." Jessie gave a shrug. He just wasn't good at the people stuff. Even Amy had given up on him. She'd needed someone who understood her and who spoke more than three words a day. Here he was, having an actual conversation...though it was starting to turn a bit personal. "Maybe the muster will be a bit of fun for him."

But people either liked the space and the lifestyle or they didn't. With no other kids interested in cattle farming, there was no one else to inherit and work the land that had been in the family for as long as anyone could remember. That would be a damn shame.

"Maybe...bit of fun for all of us." Rory smiled again. Did he ever stop smiling? No and that was what made it so hard to look away. For as long as Jessie had known Rory, he'd been single. Never even had anyone live at the house. But Jessie had heard a whisper or two from the ranch hands. Nothing that could ever be pinned down. But if a couple of guys were needing to take the edge off together, then he didn't see a problem.

But he wasn't like that. The lie had been dragged out so many times it was almost threadbare, but he refused to let it go. He didn't want to be that guy. He still had the belt scars where his father had made sure he wouldn't be that guy.

At sixteen, his schooling had been over. One school holiday, his brother had teased him about having a boyfriend—he hadn't but he'd been thinking about it a lot—and their father had overheard. He hadn't been allowed to return to boarding school after that. Steve had apologized, hadn't realized it would be an issue. It had taken five years before Jessie had even spoken to his brother again. They were okay now and Steve trusted Jessie with his boy and came down sometimes to see how the place was going. But things had never been the same between them, not even after their father died.

The white ute trundled up the dirt track in a puff of dust.

Rosie bounced around like she had unlimited energy, but she'd be asleep in the back of the ute five minutes up the road.

When the ute stopped, Baz and Mike got out. Mike's hair was flat today, not spiked up, but his jaw was set, and his gaze was surly.

"Hi, mate." Baz nodded at Rory before turning to Jessie. "We're all set."

Everyone carried water, food, a first-aid kit, a satellite phone, rifle, and something warm in case they were stuck out at night. It had only happened once in Jessie's thirty-six years, but out here when help was a million miles away, it was better to have everything on hand.

"Let's go find my cows. Last I saw them, they were northwest." Jessie doubted they'd moved on. The grass was still green and lush up there. The winter rains had been kind and they'd had a good year. The fattened cattle would fetch a good price. If every year were like this, it would make running the station extremely profitable. Instead, he was always banking the good years to cover the lean.

A few minutes later, he was in the sky. Amy had hated him flying, and not just because the insurance was diabolical—flying low and slow was dangerous—but he'd been doing it for close to twenty years. It was his favorite part of the job. If they'd been heading south, he'd have been able to see where Rory's land would butt his.

He scanned the horizon, looking for the glimmer of water that Rory claimed to have seen. He must have taken the bird up high for a bit of a joy flight before arriving. Alone, he allowed himself to smile as he remembered Rory greeting Rosie and the way he'd looked up at Jessie. Like he wanted to greet Jessie the same way. For a moment, Jessie let that idea unspool. It wasn't the first time he'd toyed with the idea, but he had no idea how to deal with it. He was old enough to know, and to know better.

Static in his ear broke the daydream. He jerked his full attention back to the job at hand.

"Boss, are you seeing this?" Baz said over the radio.

Jessie tipped the R22 and swooped lower, circling back to the ute. Rosie wasn't sleeping in the tray. She was alert, ears up. It took Jessie only a few moments to realize what Baz meant. There were dead birds dotted all over the ground.

"Yeah, I see them." He got a little lower. Must be a hundred of them. "Don't let Rosie eat any."

"Poison?" Rory's chopper approached from the other side.

What else could it be? But that meant someone had been on his land. Had they also been stealing his cattle?

"Baz, can you throw one in a bag? We'll take it home and give it to the vet."

"Sure thing."

But it was Mike that got out and bagged a sample. He flicked the bird at Jessie and held his finger up for several seconds to make his point. Jessie sighed. Mike should be grateful his dad wasn't an asshole or a bully. He pulled away to be alone with his thoughts, though today he didn't like any of them. He didn't want to remember his father and he didn't want to be thinking about Rory as anything other than a friend. But it was getting harder every time they were alone.

Thirty minutes later, Jessie saw the splash of sun on water, and some cattle grazing nearby.

"Told you there'd been flooding," Rory said, and Jessie could almost hear the smile on his lips.

Jessie was about to make a quip when something farther north else caught his eye. "What the fuck are those trees?"

"They're ferns. Mom has them in her garden," Mike said over the radio.

Jessie knew they were ferns...but why were they out here and on his land?

CHAPTER 2

The cattle were spread out beneath Jessie. Some grazed by the lake, others were in amongst the ferns that thickened the farther north Jessie looked. A few animals lifted their heads as he flew over them, surveying the situation. The station was usually green this time of year, but not ferny. In a couple of months' time, it would be brown until the next lot of rains.

He checked his position on the GPS, but was still over station land, even though he didn't recognize it. As far as he knew, there'd never been flooding in this area or ferns. He'd never seen so many dead birds either.

"What do you want to do, boss?" Baz asked over the radio.

Worry gnawed at him. He needed to figure out what was going on...would the flooding get worse? Would his cattle be next to start dying? Better to get them mustered, then he'd worry about the state of the land.

"Head north as planned and get the cattle." He'd come back another time and try to figure out what the hell was going on. Maybe a dam had burst or something. But he'd heard nothing on the news.

This was just one herd; over the next couple of days, they'd get them all rounded up, but first, he wanted to get the stragglers.

Rory buzzed over the lake. "I think you've got crocs in the water."

That wasn't possible. But then given the way the day was going, he wasn't sure about anything. He swung the R22 over the water, glad he could see the other side of the lake. It looked to be about a klick wide, and it stretched north like a silvery snake. "As long as they aren't eating cattle."

He peered down at the dark shadows moving in the water. How deep was it? He'd always though his land was reasonably flat...but the water had filled the low-lying undulation.

There were no crocs lying in the shallows or sunbathing on the shore. The creatures in the lake swam quickly, reminding him more of dolphins, but that was impossible. He lived nowhere near the ocean, and the river that ran through his property didn't have dolphins, or fish that big. So how the fuck had they gotten there? Had he slept through a hurricane that had dropped them on his land?

While the cattle were near the water, none of them were drinking from it. Maybe they were wary of the creatures too. He went a little lower, but the down draft of the blades made the water too choppy to see anything.

"I don't think they're crocs," Jessie said. Or dolphins. Were they salmon or tuna? One of the things breached the surface and stared at him with an eye the size of his palm, before its scaled body sunk back below. "Did you see that?"

"Yeah..." Rory sounded completely serious for the first time that morning.

A cool breeze swept through the cockpit as Jessie turned toward the shore. Sweat trickled down his back and he couldn't squash the bubble of fear that something was very wrong.

Rory followed him back to land. "What do you want to do?"

He had no fucking idea. He could report the flooding and see if anyone else was affected. He was going to report the bird kills. The ferns? No one would care about that unless they were some kind of invasive species he'd never heard of. "We either muster, fly north to see what's going on, or land and take a closer look? You ever heard of anything like this before?"

"No...this looks like flooding but different."

"Yeah, different." Flooding didn't usually bring ferns and dolphins. Except they weren't dolphins in the water. He was one hundred percent sure about that. They weren't snakes and they weren't crocs or turtles, or even big fish, so he wasn't sure what was left.

"Boss... There's some dead cattle."

Jessie swore under his breath and turned the R22 toward the ute. "On my way."

The ute was parked near something tall and leafy that wasn't a fern. Even though the day should've been warming up, there was a cold breeze and a bite to the air. Jessie landed and noted that at least there weren't any dead birds around.

Just dead cattle, which was worse as it took a lot more poison to kill a cow than a bird. If it was poison. Was the water some kind of toxic spill? And the animals swimming in it?

Baz waited, rifle cradled in his arm. Mike was in the ute. Rosie was on the ground, wired and sniffing everything.

Jessie raked his fingers through his hair. "Not dead of starvation or illness, I'm guessing."

"No." Baz tramped through knee-high ferns; last week there'd been no ferns—how fast did they grow? But last week there'd been no lake either. He'd flown over his property to locate the cattle and check fences, and he'd remember if there was a new lake.

Jessie followed Baz toward the dead animal.

"Can I get out of the car, Jessie?" Mike asked.

"Not yet," he called back. He didn't know what they were dealing with, and since Baz had his gun out, that meant the stockman was suitably worried.

"I'm not a kid," Mike snapped.

"You're my brother's kid." If anything happened, he'd never forgive himself. For all that Mike was a pain in the ass at the moment, he'd probably grow out of it. Hopefully, sooner rather than later.

Baz stopped and Jessie stood beside him. The remains had definitely been a cow once, but what was left was a few well-picked over bones and some hide. A cloud of flies lifted off the remaining strips of meat. Bones were scattered like puzzle pieces.

"Dingo?" Jessie asked, knowing it was a bit of wishful thinking.

Baz lifted an eyebrow. Yeah, Jessie didn't believe it either. He'd just been hopeful.

"It's all a bit odd..." Baz toed one of the ferns with his boot.

Rory tramped over, hat on, lips turned up and ready to smile. Except he didn't and Jessie was disappointed. "You've got some problems."

Jessie nodded. *Clearly.*

This wasn't the first time a dead cow had been found when mustering. It wouldn't be the last either. But it was everything else that was setting his teeth on edge. He needed to find out what was going on, so then he could work out who to call.

"I want to head north a bit and see how far this goes. See if Mac is affected too." But if he was, why hadn't he called? If something was going wrong, they let each other know. They were neighbors. And out here that meant everything. Still, it was his property and he needed to check it out. He glanced at Rory. "You right to fly north?"

Rory nodded. "Yeah. I want to see how far this spreads."

"If it hasn't flowed down to you, you're probably okay." But for how long? How fast would the ferns and bird kills spread?

"Depends on where that water is coming from and how fast it's flowing. I don't want dolphins down my way." Rory flicked him a grin.

Maybe this would be funnier if it wasn't happening on his property and therefore his problem to fix. He tipped his gaze to the sky. All he'd wanted was a good day of mustering and a few beers with Rory after so he could torment himself.

"Dolphins?" Baz frowned.

"In the lake." But Jessie was pretty damn sure they weren't dolphins. He didn't know what they were and that was worse.

"Can I get out of the car now?" Mike called, like a two-year-old that didn't take no for an answer.

Jessie turned, the kid was half out the window as it was. "No. We're heading off again." He lowered his voice and looked at Baz and Rory. "Right?"

"Your call, boss."

"Let's have a look. It won't take long, and the cattle will still be waiting for us. Plus, we need to gather any stragglers anyway," Rory said.

But before they took to the air again, Jessie strode over to the lake. The cattle milled about, munching on the ferns and other greenery but keeping a distance from the water.

Rory walked up to the edge and squatted down. His jeans hugged his ass, and Jessie had to make an effort to look away. Rory put his hand in the water before bringing it to his lips. He pulled a face and shook the water off his hand. "Salt water."

"That doesn't make sense." It didn't rain salt water. And even if it did, it hadn't rained enough to make a lake this size.

He was tempted to check for himself. He hesitated for a moment, then gave in, squatting next to Rory. Sure enough, the water was freezing cold and salty. "Well, that explains why the cattle won't drink it."

Rosie ran over, knocking into him and then Rory. Jessie ruffled her fur.

Rory's hand knocked his as he did the same, but he didn't pull away, just tossed him a smile. "We need to find out where it's coming from."

"Mac offered to buy the land last year...you don't think he'd..." but even as Jessie suggested it, he knew it was too farfetched. This wasn't a few unexplained cattle deaths, or even broken fences and stolen cattle. Besides that, Mac had asked just about everyone around. Not just him.

"You can't sell to him...I like you as my neighbor." Rory clapped him on the shoulder then stood. "Come on. We may not get any mustering done today, but we can at least solve this and alert the appropriate people."

Jessie took another look at the lake. Sunlight danced over the surface and he shuddered. It might be pretty, but it didn't belong here.

The thought worried at him as he got back in the chopper and took to the sky. But where had it come from? Had it bubbled up? His property had flooded before...just not with salt water. Maybe the salt had washed in from somewhere.

And the things in the water were probably massive fish, that's all. Fish that would feed them for weeks and fill up the freezer. Of course, they'd have to come back out with rods and tackle—not that he had either.

He'd never fished before, but it would be a waste to not give it a try.

Jessie tilted the chopper and checked in on the ute, still trundling through the knee-high ferns, reminding him that it wasn't just the saltwater lake that was wrong. "See anything else odd down there?"

"Nah," Baz said.

There was a muted discussion then Mike came on the radio. "Another dead cow, still meaty."

"Hmm. Keep your eyes out. Could be a pack of feral dogs." And those packs could get big. Ferals making a home on his land was the last thing he needed. But they had been known to roam out here, usually taking calves and sheep. But they could take down an adult cow when working as a team. If that were the case, he'd have to call in a licensed catcher. That seemed like the easy answer. He almost relaxed, glad to have one problem solved.

He glanced at Rosie in the tray of the ute and wished she was riding with him, just in case they ran into feral dogs. He let her in the R22 when they were just heading out to check on the fences and the cattle, and he'd even bought her a harness so she wouldn't be able to jump out and hurt herself.

Rory swept past him.

To Jessie's left, the lake seemed to stretch forever. The ferns gave way to trees and it didn't feel like the land he'd grown up on. It was alien, like he was flying somewhere else. Was that a damn pine tree?

This was getting too weird. But who was going to care that trees had suddenly sprouted or that there was a saltwater lake on his property? They were his problems. And he had no idea how to deal with them. Nothing his father had taught him had covered this. But then, none of what his father had taught him had prepared him for life beyond drinking, shouting, and swearing.

Rory's chopper jerked and dropped. Jessie's heart lurched. Then the chopper recovered.

"Rory, what do you see up there?"

All he got back was static. *Fuck.* But the little R22 was still flying. Rory was okay. Jessie checked below on the ute.

The ute followed a trail in the ferns, vanishing for seconds beneath the leaves. Every time it was out of sight, Jessie held his breath. He wanted to turn back but they hadn't reached the northern boundary of the station yet.

"Baz, any sign of my cattle?"

"There's a few. It's a bit green here, boss."

That was an understatement.

Before he could reply, his chopper gave a wobble like it hit a pocket of air. His grip tightened as the R22 dropped several meters, and his skids brushed the tree canopy. He pulled up as sweat blistered on his back. Before him was not just a few trees but an entire forest.

CHAPTER 3

Jessie stared at the forest, not sure where it had come from or why it was here. There were definitely pine trees and they definitely didn't belong. A cold breeze swept into the cockpit, drawing up the hairs on his bare forearms.

He tried the radio again. "Rory, can you hear me?"

"I hear you. Lost you for a bit in the turbulence."

Jessie checked the sat nav, but it had no signal. He gave it a couple of taps. Nothing.

The ute broke out from under the canopy and stopped about five meters from the edge of the lake...the lake that now stretched as far as he could see. This kind of flooding should've been on the news. A forest appearing should've been noticed by more than just him. Yet he'd heard nothing, not even whispered gossip.

He flew along the shoreline to where twenty cattle grazed. Were they as confused as him or just enjoying the lush greens?

Over the lake, several large birds flew.

Below him, the water was crystal clear, making it impossible to guess at the depth. Something that looked like a turtle swam in the shallows. He went a little farther over the water, high enough that he didn't make ripples. Close enough that he could see fish and the dolphin things, and other creatures with impossibly long necks. For several heartbeats, he just stared, not sure what he was seeing. He should be able to name the animals and he couldn't, not without using words that didn't belong.

This was too weird. He turned the chopper 180 degrees, to face back the way he'd come and lifted higher into the air. The ute was still there, waiting on the shore. Rory was hovering over the forest. But beyond the other chopper, all Jessie could see was more lake and more forest disappearing into the horizon. It was like his stretch of shrub and grass didn't exist. He swallowed hard. He should've been able to see his cattle and the flat grassland they'd been standing on only minutes ago.

"Jessie, watch your right," Rory urged.

Jessie glanced over in time to see that the birds weren't birds at all. They were massive, featherless beasts. Two of them attacked the R22. The engine revved, trying to keep up with extra weight. One creature fell away, bleeding from where the blades had clipped it and hit the water with a splash. The chopper lurched as the damaged blades couldn't keep it airborne.

Jessie cursed and angled toward the shore, not wanted to pitch in deep water—not wanting to go down at all. The remaining thing stuck its head in the open cockpit and started attacking him with its toothed beak. It snapped at his arms and legs.

He needed both hands to keep the chopper up.

The weight of the thing was unbalancing the chopper and dragging him down. The R22 turned and tilted as Jessie fought for control.

The creature—not a bird, not a bat; he didn't want to name it because it was impossible—latched onto his arm and bit. Its teeth sunk into his flesh and it tugged at him like it wanted to rip him out of the cockpit. The harness kept him strapped to his seat, but the creature was going to take his arm off.

His headphones were filled with yelling. Rory and Baz telling him what he already knew. He was fucked, but he couldn't spare a second to tell them to shut up so he could think, so he ripped the headset off and threw it at the creature jerking on his arm. It didn't let go. The chopper dropped as another one landed on the skids and stuck its head through the other side of the cockpit.

This was it. He was going to die, getting ripped apart by dinosaurs.

Jessie kicked at the one trying to rip his arm off. It let go with a screech. Jessie wrestled with the controls, keeping the shallows by the shore as his goal. The water beneath him became choppy with the downdraft.

The crack of a rifle cut through the noise of the whining chopper and the snapping and honking of the dinosaurs. The dinosaur that had been chewing on his arm pulled away.

The R22 gave a shudder and all Jessie could do was try and make it to the shallow water and get as low as possible to reduce the impact. If he was lucky, he'd kiss the water and sink gently before tipping over. If he was unlucky, he'd hit the water hard and at a bad angle. The engine groaned. The remaining dinosaur snapped, narrowly missing his other arm. He risked letting go with one hand so he could reach behind and grab a weapon. His fingers closed over the sat phone. He smacked it into the creature's eye. It glared at him as though shocked he'd had the audacity to fight back.

"I'm not good eating, asshole."

But that didn't stop it from trying again.

The water churned as something, or several somethings, attacked the fallen dinosaur. The shore was too far away...ten meters might as well be forever. His skids were barely over the waves of his downdraft. This was it.

"I'm going down in dino-infested water." It was obvious, but he had to say it out loud to make it real. If he made it to shore, it would be a bloody miracle. He wished he'd had the chance to tell Mike he was a good kid, instead of just ragging on him for being on his phone instead of helping out. His throat tightened. He should've had the balls to tell Rory the real reason why Amy had left and that he'd fancied him from the day they'd met.

The icy water closed around his legs. The flying dinosaur left him to go under alone. He drew in a breath before the water closed over his head and the helicopter rolled over, dragged down by the weight of the blades and engine.

It was then he opened his eyes and unclipped the harness. The things that had been behind him in the chopper now floated past. The cooler and his jacket and hat. He wanted to waste a few seconds grabbing the rifle and his food, but he needed his hands free to swim. The first-aid kit was held in place with straps and he didn't have time to undo it. Already his lungs were aching, and the cold was seeping into his bones. He pulled himself out of the cockpit, the blades already resting on the sandy seafloor. The surface was only a couple of kicks away. He sucked in air and located the shore. Baz was thigh-deep, rifle at the ready. Rory was landing his R22 nearby.

Jessie swam like he was back in year ten and trying to win the hundred-meter freestyle. He usually came close to last, but this had to be a personal best. He couldn't look behind him, not even when Baz fired the rifle. When his feet hit the bottom of the lake, he ran with water-logged boots, wet jeans, and shirt—worse than any late for school race.

Rory ran past Baz to haul him the rest of the way out.

Something smacked into the back of his legs and he stumbled into Rory's arms. The rifle cracked again. The bullet hissed past and into the water.

Rory held him steady, and half-carried, half-dragged him out of the water, while Jessie coughed and shivered and wanted nothing more than to sink to the gritty sand on the shore.

Rory kept him upright. "You had us a bit worried, mate."

"I'm fine," he said through chattering teeth. The water was freezing cold and filled with dinosaurs. He was not fine at all, but he didn't know how to say it without sounding like he'd lost his mind.

Rory kept his arm around him, a warm solid presence that was far too comforting. For a moment, he wanted to lean closer. Instead, he knocked Rory's hand away in case he forgot himself or the others noticed that he was enjoying the attention. As it was, Jessie made the mistake of lifting his gaze. The concern was evident in Rory's eyes. The usual almost smile had been completely erased. The things Jessie couldn't talk about were rising to the surface.

He turned away on shaky legs. The danger wasn't just in the water.

His heart beat fast like the blades of a chopper. His R22 was visible through the blood-stained water. He kept his teeth locked together so they didn't chatter. There were supplies down there that they needed; his sat phone, his rifle.

No one was going in there to get them. He shook his head. He was never going to be able to claim the loss of the helicopter on his insurance. Who would believe him?

"Mike, bring the first-aid kit," Rory called.

"He should stay in the ute. It's not safe and I'm fine." Jessie cut Rory a glare. "Stop worrying about me." His words came out too gruff.

"You're bleeding. Given the situation..."

"It's not a situation. There are dinosaurs out there. Now I may only be a stock hand who never finished school, but dinosaurs are long dead. So... So...what the hell?" Baz scanned the water and then the beach and the tree line.

They were exposed. Four little humans and one dog.

Where was Rosie?

Jessie gave a whistle and she came bolting out of the trees. She knocked into his legs and licked his fingers and that was when he noticed the blood running down his arm and dripping on the sand. Rory's worry made brutal sense.

The gouges left by the flying thing's teeth had ripped open his skin. The cuts were ragged and deep, like he'd tangled with a feral dog. He rocked on his feet, needing to sit.

Rory caught his elbow. "Maybe you should take a moment and rest."

Yeah, maybe he should. Where he'd been standing, there was blood scattered all over the sand. "We should leave. You can patch me up when we…" When they what? Got home? Where was home? Where were they? "When we get back to the station."

Rory pressed his lips together. "I'd rather not have you dripping blood and making us prey."

That was a very good point, but they should leave now. Go back the way they came, and they'd be home. Wouldn't they? "The longer we spend here, the more dangerous. Let's just pack up and go."

"Which would be a whole lot easier if the GPS worked," Baz said. "Got no idea where we are."

"Or when," Rory added. His eyebrows knitted in a rare scowl.

"Uncle Jess." Mike gave him a quick hug. The teen looked like he was about to cry. "There's a lot of blood."

"I'll be fine, kid." He slapped Mike's shoulder with his good hand, but even that was smeared with blood.

Mike's eyes were wide. "The pterosaur nearly had you. There were four of them, all attacking the R22. And they were huge." He spread his arms, but their wingspan had been bigger than that.

He frowned at Mike. "Pterosaur? You know what those things are?"

Mike had often spent his school holidays looking for fossils and talking about long-dead things. Jessie had half-listened, more worried about the living.

"Yeah...there used to be a sea that covered a chunk of inland Australia. I used to find little ammonite fossils when I'd come to visit."

"I thought they were just rocks." He'd never thrown them out because they were Mike's rock collection. They were still in a box in Mike's room as far as Jessie knew.

"Eromanga Sea," Rory said, taking the first-aid kit from Mike. "I remember going some school excursion."

"That's the one." Mike nodded. "Maybe we're still on the station, but somehow we..." his voice faltered.

"We went back in time," Jessie said, knowing he sounded like he'd lost his mind, or banged his head in the crash. Maybe he was dead. Though why his afterlife would be filled with dinosaurs he wasn't sure.

Rory took Jessie's hand and held his arm out then doused it in antiseptic.

"Ow." The open wounds burned. He tried to yank his arm away, but Rory held tight. His rough hands were used to handling half-ton cattle, so keeping a hold of Jessie was no trouble.

"The cuts are deep and who knows what infection you might pick up," Rory said.

"Back in time...that explains the dinosaurs," Baz said with a nod as if that made perfect sense.

"That doesn't explain anything." Mike raked his fingers through his hair, making it spike up like he was a wannabe punk. "How did we get here?"

"Well, we drove, and they flew," Baz said like it was funny. No one laughed.

"Mike's right. How did we get here? And how did the ferns and the water end up on my land?"

Rory started bandaging Jessie's arm. He was silent when he'd usually have a bit to say. His lips were pressed together in a line, not a smile.

"Rory?" Jessie pressed.

"Well, since we've suspended all ties to sanity and reality...I think it was a rip in time." He smiled but it was forced, showing too many teeth.

"So we just go back through the rip." It sounded so easy. But without GPS, would they be able to find it again? Jessie wished he hadn't insisted on going north to see the extent of the damage. They could've mustered the cattle that were there, and he could've made some phone calls... And at some point, he'd have gone to investigate, probably on his own.

He glanced at Baz, Mike, and Rory, and while he regretted dragging them into this mess, he was glad to have them with him.

Mike shook his head. "If it were a rip, that doesn't explain the plants on our side. And unless sci-fi TV shows have been lying to me, we should be able to see the tear...what if it closes and we're stuck?"

"Stop. We don't need to know the why or the how about arriving, only how to leave." Jessie shivered. His wet clothes were sucking all the heat out of him.

Rory used a clip to hold the bandage in place and released Jessie's hand. He missed the rough grip immediately and buried that feeling with the rest of them.

"When I turned, all I saw was more forest and more water." Rory shook his head and glanced up at the clear blue sky. "Mike's right. I didn't see a tear when we came through. What if there is no way back?"

CHAPTER 4

"I didn't see a rip either. Just more forest and sea," Jessie said quietly. It had terrified him. The familiar rolls of his property had vanished. He didn't want to be trapped millions of years in the past. He had a home, and a life—well, he had a living. The cattle wouldn't miss him. But he had to get Mike back. The mood of the group sank like the R22 and was probably just as unrecoverable.

"I'm not quitting that easily," Baz said.

"I didn't say I was quitting," Jessie said. "Just that it's not obvious and I think we need a plan."

Rory blew out a breath. "I can take a quick flight, but if those pterosaurs bring me down over the trees, it won't be as pretty as Jessie's landing."

It would be fatal, and the pterosaurs would probably rip Rory apart and eat him for dinner. Dread swelled in Jessie's stomach. They would all die out here and no one would ever know what had happened to them. He could've died. His gaze drifted to where the Eromanga Sea lapped at the shore. He'd known it wasn't fucking dolphins or crocodiles in the lake on his land. Mike would probably know what they were, not that naming them would change anything.

Jessie blew out a breath. "Agreed. No flying. I also think we should stay together. All my supplies are underwater." He nodded at Rory. "Do you want to get yours and put them in the ute?"

"Worried someone's going to pinch them?" Rory grinned.

"Not all dinosaurs were big. There'll be small scavengers who'll investigate and get into your food." Mike turned around, scanning the area with wide eyes. For a few moments, he was the kid he'd once been, excited by small rocks and puppies. "We don't even know what lives around here."

"Dino-possums?" Jessie asked hopefully. He could live without seeing a *T-rex*.

Mike shrugged. "Yeah, maybe? No one knows. It's all best guesses based on bits of bone. There might be big ones too."

Everyone turned to stare at the tree line, as though expecting something to make an appearance on cue.

"I'm going to unload the chopper." Rory took a few steps in that direction, away from the trees.

"I'll go with you," Baz said.

Jessie watched them walk the twenty meters away; not far, but here it seemed like forever. Beyond them were the cows. How many of his herd had wandered through? If he found a way back home, would he come back for them, or leave them to be dino dinner?

"How's your arm?"

"Fine, kid. It was just some scratches." Scratches that were big enough and deep enough that he should be getting stitches. But he didn't need to trouble Mike. The best thing he could do was get him talking about the dinos. "So, what do you reckon lives in the sea?"

"What did you see?"

"Dolphins with big eyes, about five meters long."

"Long neck?"

"No, these ones were in the water at home."

"Probably ichthyosaurs." Mike frowned and stared at the sea. "If that is Eromanga, then the giant *Kronosaurus* lives in there."

It might not be the Eromanga Sea, but given they had no other best guesses, that's what Jessie was going with. "How big is giant?"

"Like a bus."

Jessie was infinitely glad he hadn't flown out farther over the sea. If he'd been well offshore when the pterosaurs had attacked, he'd have been eaten, if not by the ichthyosaurs then by the *Kronosaurus*. Neither of which were appealing.

"I want to get some photos of dinosaurs. No one is going to believe this." Mike pulled his phone out of his pocket. "I've got no signal."

"No shit. 4G hasn't been invented yet."

"Oh yeah." His smile brightened. "Camera still works though." He took a photo of the water and the drowned R22. Then turned to take another of Baz and Rory, making their way to the ute with their arms full of supplies.

"Time to go." He put a hand on his nephew's shoulder and guided him toward the cab of the ute. Blood seeped through Jessie's bandage. Any predator would smell the wounded prey a mile away. But there was nothing he could do about it.

Baz and Rory dropped the supplies into the crate on the tray of the ute.

"I had a shirt and a pair of shorts in the back, thought you might want something." Rory held out the clothing.

Jessie's first instinct was to refuse simply because they were Rory's, but the last thing he needed was a dose of hypothermia to go with the blood loss. "Thanks."

He pulled his wet T-shirt over his head, and tossed it in the tray, then slipped on Rory's blue checked shirt. It smelled faintly of dog and fuel and sweat, like he'd worn it and tossed it in the back of the chopper. He wanted to breathe it in, but instead did the buttons up as quick as he could so he could pretend he wasn't affected.

As uncomfortable as the wet jeans were, putting on Rory's shorts would be a bit too personal. He glanced over; Rory was grinning like he knew exactly what Jessie was thinking. It was almost enough for him to refuse, but then Rory would know that Jessie had been thinking about the implications of wearing the offered shorts.

"If you could give me a moment?" Jessie undid his belt and waited for Rory and Baz to turn their backs. When they did, he undid his boots and stepped out of them, so he could peel off his jeans. He pulled the shorts on. They were a little loose, and shorter than Jessie liked. These were best suited to running around and playing footy. He'd seen Rory wearing a similar pair at a BBQ one time. Amy had been with him, but he'd been distracted. He shoved his boots back on, knowing that he needed to get out of the wet socks as soon as possible, then he chucked his jeans and belt in the back of the ute.

He gave Rosie a whistle and she ran back from the cattle. Even here, she was ready to do her job. She jumped on to the tray without needing a second invitation. Mike was already in the cab, which was the best place for him, even though the door was open, and he was scrolling through his phone. But the ute only fitted two in the cabin. While that had seemed adequate when Jessie had purchased it about five years ago, it now seemed like a rather large oversight.

"I'll sit in the back." Jessie put his hand out for the rifle Baz was holding.

"Like hell. You're already bleeding. Get in the cab and drive."

Jessie glanced at Rory for support, but Rory shook his head. "I'm with him, get in the cab."

"Baz, you know the route you took."

Baz glanced at the ground and scuffed a toe in the sand. "Mostly. I wasn't expecting it to disappear the moment my back was turned."

Jessie swore. He hadn't watched the ute's path either. He'd kept one eye on the ute and the other on the trees and changing landscape.

"I've got it, Uncle Jess." Mike pulled out his phone and showed the video of the ute going from the fern-littered scrub and then onto the trail between the trees.

All they had to do was follow the route back. There was only one problem. "Your phone's on thirty-four percent."

"I've got a power pack in my bag." Mike's grin faded a little. "I know you hate me taking my phone everywhere..."

"I'm glad you did." Jessie smiled.

Jessie and Mike got into the cabin while Baz and Rory climbed into the back with Rosie and the rifles. They were leaving both R22s and the cattle. He looked in the rearview mirror and hesitated. Neither belonged here. Someone tapped the roof of the cab to let Jessie know they were ready. His gaze landed on Rory in the rearview mirror for just a second.

It was wrong to be wearing his shorts... Jessie glanced down at his bare thighs. But he was damn glad to be out the wet jeans. He was warmer already.

Mike turned and glanced back. "Are you worried about your cows?"

"Yeah." That was all he was thinking about.

"We can come back...you have a portal to the past on your land. People will pay you for this. Scientists will want to study the portal and the dinosaurs." Mike's eyes were bright, and he spoke fast. "I wanted to be an archaeologist for like, forever. Now I could study actual living dinosaurs."

"You might need to finish school for that." Jessie started the car. Maybe this would be the kick Mike needed to get his shit together. "Right, let's look for landmarks on the video and get out of here." He hoped he sounded more confident than he felt.

They followed the trail through the trees. On the ground, it was vastly different to the view he'd had. The shadows were denser, the trees and shrubs could be hiding anything. Well, not anything but dinosaurs. His window was down, and every rustle made him glance over.

The rich scent of decaying vegetation and pine filled his lungs. This wasn't the Australian bush he was used to. It wasn't even the far north rainforest. It was ancient and untouched. He didn't want hordes of scientists coming through and damaging it. Worse, miners and loggers coming through to strip what they could from the past. Big game hunters and fishers....

What changes would ripple through to the present? Had they already done something that would change the future?

"Left here," Mike said.

"Are you sure it's left?" Jessie peered at the screen.

"Yeah, that tree," Mike pointed to the one almost in front of them, "is this one." He pointed at the screen.

"Okay."

"Can you make this trip a little quicker? I think we have curious followers," Rory called out.

Jessie turned down the fork. This time, he was paying attention to the trees. He was noticing the broken branches and the claw marks. Something lived in the forest and he wasn't in a rush to meet it. All he wanted to do was get home and make some calls and get rid of the past that was intruding on his property.

"Keep going until you see the fallen tree then jag right," Mike said, calm as though navigating through ancient forest was his favorite pastime.

Jessie turned right at the fallen tree that was almost as high as the car.

"The trees should start to thin and..." Mike looked up. "We should be seeing home."

Jessie stopped the ute, dread swelling in his gut. The trees hadn't thinned. In the mottled light, the trail continued through the forest.

"Let me have a look at the video." He put his hand out for the phone.

Mike stared out the windscreen. "But we did it right. We should be home. Maybe we need to drive a bit farther."

Jessie took the phone out of Mike's hand and studied the video. They were in the right spot. He scanned the area, looking for even a glimmer of home, or any sign of a tear. "It's okay, we'll figure it out."

Rosie started barking.

"We've got company," Baz said.

The trees shook and knee-high beakless chickens with whip-like tails swarmed the trail, squawking and squeaking and carrying on. Jessie couldn't see what was going on behind the ute, but thirty ran in front.

"Did you record it?" Mike snatched his phone out of Jessie's hand.

"No." But it didn't matter, as Mike was already leaning out the window catching the tail end of the flock. "That was cool, but I'm still ready to go home."

Jessie checked Rory and Baz were still sitting then inched the ute forward, holding his breath, hoping that something would change. In the R22, he'd hit turbulence. That had been the moment he'd crossed. "What did it feel like when you went through the time rip?"

"I think my ears popped? I wasn't paying that much attention. I was too busy filming. It was all so weird." Mike glanced out the window. "Why isn't it changing?"

They were about ten meters past the fallen tree now and there was no sign of the forest ending. Jessie sighed and stopped the ute. He closed his eyes. All he wanted to do was swear and scream. If Mike hadn't been with him, he might've given in to the temptation.

"There's no way back, is there?" Mike whispered.

"Maybe it moves," Jessie said.

"Then how do we find it?"

"I don't know," Jessie shouted and regretted it immediately. He lowered his voice. "I don't know, okay?"

Mike stared at him. "It's not my fault."

"I didn't say it was. You did great with the video. You and Baz should've never investigated the ferns. I should've gone alone."

"Then you'd be stuck here by yourself."

Yeah, but that was better than dragging the people he cared about with him.

"At least we can figure this out together. Besides, we all wanted to know what was going on." Mike frowned. "I'd have never guessed dinosaurs though."

"And look where curiosity got us."

They both stared out the windscreen.

"Are you lost?" Baz called.

Jessie got out of the ute, the ferns brushing his bare legs. His jeans wouldn't be dry yet, unfortunately. "No, worse. We should be standing in my paddock. The portal or rip or whatever should've been about ten meters back." He pointed up the trail.

Rory and Baz both turned to look behind them.

"So where is it?" Rory said.

"I don't know." He looked at his watch. "We've been here less than two hours..." And he was already injured. "We need to make a plan."

"Wait for a bit and see if something changes?" Rory asked.

Rosie stood and barked. Her hackles rose and the bark became a snarl. Rory and Baz lifted their rifles. The forest whispered and rustled. Insects hummed through the branches, and screeches and honks and clicks filled the air. The occasional bird flitted through the trees.

"Settle, girl." Jessie reached over the side of the tray and patted her, but she ignored him. Her gaze intent on something else.

A dinosaur the size of a man burst out of the trees next to the ute, saw them, startled, and ran down the trail toward the beach.

Rory's shoulder's sagged and he lowered the rifle. "At least it ran away."

Baz and Rosie were both still on alert.

"I'm going to back up to the fork. Can you mark it if I stop?"

"Yeah." Rory nodded. "Let's not lose this place. Maybe the door home only opens at certain times."

"Good thinking." Jessie smiled. But at what time did it open? If it opened.

"We aren't camping here," Baz grumbled. "Not unless we sleep up in the trees."

Jessie glanced up as he got back into the car. He'd never been much of climber.

Carefully, he reversed up the trail until he reached the fork. Rory jumped out of the back and slashed an arrow pointing left down the correct fork. Jessie could just see the fallen tree that was close to where the crossing point should be. Every time he blinked, he willed the scenery to be different. For the trees to have vanished.

"Are we going to have lunch and keep trying?" Mike asked.

"That's as good a plan as any, kid." He wasn't going to sit here and quit.

Rosie barked again. If she was going to bark at every dinosaur, it was going to get old fast. Jessie threw open the door and got out to go and shut her up. Rory had his rifle trained on the trail. It might be the same dino or it might be a different one—they looked the same—but this time, it was running straight toward them. Another popped out of the trees on the other side of the ute.

"Put your window up!" Jessie shouted at Mike. He had no doubt that his nephew would be recording everything until his phone went flat.

The dino's head snapped around to stare at him. Five meters and a ute between him and the dino wasn't nearly enough. He didn't know much about dinosaurs, but he knew enough that pointy teeth meant meat-eater—somethings hadn't changed that much over the millennia. This one was a dingy green-blue color with darker stripes. Its limbs were long and thin and its hands, if they could be called that, had long fingers and longer claws. The dino looked too delicate to be a predator.

The bark of a rifle dragged Jessie's attention back to the other dino. It was staring, unafraid of the men or the noise. Baz let off another round, the second shot finding its mark, and the dino crumbled mid-charge.

Next to him, Rory was still watching the one on the other side of the cab, rifle at the ready. "We're going to run out of bullets before we run out of dinos."

The living dino bellowed and ran around to its friend. It sniffed and nudged at the body the way a cow might wonder about its suddenly still buddy. The dino made a few soft noises, as though to encourage the dead one to get up. When the dead didn't rise, it turned its attention back to the humans.

Rosie put her paws up on the edge of the tray and barked and snarled like she could take it on.

Jessie whistled, trying to get her to calm down. She growled and paced toward him and for a moment, Jessie thought the dino was going to walk away and Rosie was going to behave.

Then the dino yipped like it was a dog and Rosie raced back to the end of the tray to bark. Jessie willed Baz to just shoot it, but they couldn't waste bullets and it wasn't attacking. Its head tilted as though studying them. Then it bolted into the trees like it had decided that humans were too much trouble.

No one moved for what felt like hours. Jessie's muscles were tight, and his heart was stampeding. "I need to drag the dino off the trail."

"I'll help." Rory put his rifle in the tray.

"I've got you covered," Baz said.

Jessie couldn't help but watch the trees as he covered the few meters to the body. For a moment, he just looked at it. It had long emu-like legs; bet it didn't make nice steak though.

Rory used the toe of his boot to give its haunch a nudge.

The dino didn't twitch. It was only then Jessie relaxed and he forced a laugh. "Did you think it was going to jump up and get you?"

"Did you?" There was a glint of mischief in Rory's eyes.

For a moment, Jessie couldn't look away. He nodded. "Just a little."

They both stared at the dead dino. Its claws were wicked long, hooked and dark. Should they be taking samples? What were they going to store them in...more importantly carrying bits of dead dino seemed like a way to attract more. Not that he was superstitious.

Rory ran his finger over a front claw like he'd been thinking the same thing, but his gaze was on Jessie. "Shirt looks good on you."

Jessie squatted down, ready to drag the dino off the trail. He couldn't do this now. "Thanks for the change."

"How's your arm?"

"Fine." It clearly wasn't when there was blood seeping through the bandage, and it stung like hell. But he wasn't hurt enough that he couldn't drag a dinosaur the size of a large roo off the trail.

"I'll look at it again in a bit. Maybe I can do a better job since we aren't racing home for dinner." Rory squatted down on the other side of the dino.

Jessie glanced over. "I said it's fine." He didn't want Rory fussing over him because he might start to like it more than he should. "Did you see the way the other one reacted to this one's death?"

"Like it cared?"

"Yeah." He put his hand on the dino's tail, surprised to find it was warm to touch like a blue tongue lizard that had been lying in the sun. "It's not right."

He could accept cows mourning but not dinosaurs. Snakes and lizards didn't have feelings, and dinos were just jumped-up reptiles.

"Just because you don't care about anyone, you don't think dinosaurs can? They might mate for life. No one actually knows."

"We going to lift this or talk about feelings?" It was easier not to acknowledge them. If he did, then he might act on them.

"You admitting to having some?" Rory grinned. The corners of his eyes crinkled. "I can do both. Can you?"

Rosie saved Jessie by jumping out of the ute to help. She sniffed the body and Jessie pushed her away. He didn't want her catching something from licking the dino, or even eating it and then throwing up all over the place.

"I'm not doing this," Jessie said as he went to heft the dino. He almost stumbled and fell on his ass. The dino didn't weigh as much as a roo. It was light for the size. He could've dragged it clear of the trail by himself, but Rory still helped. They dropped the carcass by a tree and stood.

Rory wiped his hands on his jeans. "I am. The way I see it, we'll all be dead within a week if we don't get back, so I want to make myself clear. No regrets and all that."

"No." Jessie shook his head. He didn't want to hear that the attraction was shared, because then it would be harder to resist. And he didn't want to imagine being stuck here for the rest of his life—which wouldn't be that long if Rory was right.

"Tell me I'm wrong." Rory put his hands on his hips. "That there's nothing between us."

Jessie wanted to open his mouth and do just that, but the words didn't form. He couldn't lie. Yet he was running out of places to hide. He'd always liked Rory too much. Amy had seen it. Rory had noticed and was more than flattered. Had everyone else? Did they all think he was one of those guys? He turned away and started back to the ute. With a whistle, he called Rosie to his side.

Rory wasn't offended. He was interested. He was gay and didn't give a shit what people thought. Jessie stopped and closed his eyes. It would be nice to be that brave. All he'd had to do was agree there was something.

Rosie barked, and Jessie's blood ran cold.

CHAPTER 5

Jessie turned in time to see an emu-dino dive out of the trees. The creature snatched Rosie up, its claws sinking into her rust and white mottled fur.

Rosie's snarls became yelps.

"Put her down!" Jessie ran toward where the dino played with his dog like she was a toy for ripping apart. Blood sprayed as the dino tore into her and her yelps became anguished cries.

Rory grabbed him before he could reach her. He manhandled Jessie toward the ute, and Jessie fought him every step, pushing forward while Rory shoved back.

"Let me go." Jessie needed to get to Rosie.

"Get down and give me a shot, you damn fools," Baz yelled.

Rory slammed them both into the ground like a rugby tackle gone wrong. Jessie's back hit the dirt and the air left his lungs. The shot went over their heads and for several seconds there was silence, and Jessie forgot himself. Rory was pressed against him in all wrong...maybe right...places and staring down at him. Jessie couldn't breathe. Then Rosie whimpered and Jessie remembered why he was on the ground. He shoved Rory off him and scrambled up and over to Rosie. She was still in the clutches of the dino, but the dino wasn't moving. A bullet to the forehead had stopped it cold.

"Rosie, girl." His voice broke. He wanted to pat her but didn't know where. There was blood gushing out of her and pooling in the dirt, intestines poked out of the tear in her belly.

She whimpered. Her eyes wide and rolling back to look at him as though begging him for help. To make it right. Jessie's vision blurred as he smoothed his hand over the top of her head. He pulled a claw out of her, hoping to ease her pain, but that seemed to only make it worse as blood flowed from the now open wound. She whined through her nose. She was dying and he couldn't do damn thing about it. She needed a vet. But even if they were at home, he'd never get her there in time. Here, she stood no chance. He kept his hand on her head and whispered to her. Telling her that she was a good dog.

He knew what he needed to do, but Rosie was his best mate. She'd been there before he'd started dating Amy and then through the divorce. Without her, he'd be lost.

He swallowed around the lump in his throat. "I'll be back in a moment, girl."

He stood; Rory was already walking toward him with the rifle. Jessie gritted his teeth to keep from cursing him out. In that moment, he fucking hated Rory. The way he was so confident in his skin, and the way he knew what needed to be done. And while Jessie knew it wasn't Rory's fault, he needed someone to blame besides himself. He should've put Rosie in the cab with Mike and kept them both safe.

"Do you want me to?" Rory said softly.

It was a kind offer—putting down animals was hard—but Jessie glared at him as fiercely as he could. Hoping that it would be easy to turn desire into hate. However, the tear that escaped and rolled down his cheek broke his resolve. He shook his head, hating only himself.

"No." He took the offered rifle and knelt next to Rosie. "You're a good girl. The best." He kissed the top of her head.

She tried to wag her tail and whimpered instead. He was sure she knew what was coming because when he stood, she lowered her head and closed her eyes.

Jessie drew in a breath. He'd done this plenty of times before. Leaving her to suffer would be cruel. He blinked to clear his vision. He knew all of that, but it still took him several breaths before he could raise the rifle and make the shot.

Rory pulled the dinosaur's claws out of her while Jessie stood there unable to move. "Do you want me to put her in the tray of the ute?"

He wanted to take her home, but they couldn't be carting her around. "She'll attract predators. It would be best to bury her."

He bent down and picked her up like she was still living. Her body was hot like she was sleeping not dead, but his hands were sticky with blood. His knees weakened and all he wanted to do was collapse and give into the despair that the same fate was waiting for all of them if they didn't get home.

He'd dealt with floods and droughts and years when the farm was in danger of going under. But this...going into the past and dinosaurs...this was too much.

He was going to wake up in hospital. Maybe he'd crashed the R22 and he was in a coma, or there were doctors fighting to save his life and this was his brain's way of processing the trauma and helping him fight. If it was, his mind was doing a terrible job because he wanted to quit and die.

"I need the shovel, Baz," Jessie said as he walked past the ute. He was going to bury her at the fork. When, if, he got back home, would her bones still be there, buried deep and turned to stone?

Baz jumped down with the shovel in one hand and the rifle in the other. "I'm sorry I wasn't quick enough. Damn thing came out of nowhere."

"It's not your fault." His throat was thick, making talking hard.

Mike slid over and opened the door. "What happened?"

"The dino's mate got her." There was nothing he could say. The emu-dinos either hunted in pairs or mated for life. Either option was bad for them, as it meant they had to kill both to be safe.

"She's dead?" Mike's face paled.

"Yeah, kid." Rosie was dead. If they didn't find a way home, they'd all be dead too. Rory was right about that, but Jessie gave them days, not a whole week. Rory was too kind and generous.

Mike slithered out of the car and put his hand on her like he needed to be sure. "I'm sorry, Uncle Jess."

"It's okay." It wasn't. Every time he blinked, his eyes burned and his vision blurred, but he wasn't going start bawling like a two year old who'd dropped their ice cream.

Mike hugged him and Rosie. His eyes were glassy, and he sniffed before speaking. "I remember when you got her. You told me not to baby her because she was a working dog."

That summer, Mike and Rosie had been inseparable. The next summer, Rosie had been working, and doing well, but she'd remembered her playmate and had been beside herself with joy. She'd damn near wagged her tail off.

She'd never taken well to Amy. He should've paid attention, but he'd wanted it to work out. To prove that there was nothing wrong with him. And for a bit, it had. They'd had a few happy years. Even when they'd split, it hadn't been bitter, but it had been devastating. Amy had seen through him and figured out the truth.

For how many years did he live a lie out of fear?

He had to put Rosie down to dig the hole. Rory's shirt was now stained with her blood. As he worked, a dragonfly the size of his hand drifted by to see what was going on. He ignored it, and the pain in his arm. Digging gave him something to do.

But every rustle in the shrubs made him tense, even though Baz and Rory stood guard with the rifles. He paused to shake out his arm, aware that fresh blood was seeping through the bandage like he'd ripped the wounds open further. Mike took the shovel out of his hand and took over.

As much as he didn't like it, he was going to have to let Rory look at it and do a better job of keeping him together. An open wound here would kill him if the dinosaurs didn't. A small manic laugh threatened to bubble up and break free. He swallowed it, but he knew it wouldn't stay down for much longer.

Rory ended up digging the last bit of the hole, making it nice and deep. He tossed the shovel out. "Did you want to pass Rosie down to me?"

Jessie nodded and carefully handed her over. Rory gently placed her at the bottom of the hole. It didn't seem right to be leaving her here all by herself. Millions of years from home.

Jessie offered his hand, to help Rory out of the hole, because it was the right thing to do. And because he'd been a dick when Rory had been only offering kindness. Rory hesitated for a moment, as if he was aware that every movement and every word could now be misconstrued, before clasping Jessie's hand.

They'd always gotten on, been able to talk about anything. Except the thing between them that had existed from the first time they'd met. Amy had seen it, even though he'd denied it before eventually admitting that he'd always liked guys. He'd spent twenty years trying not to.

For what? To appease the ghost of his father? To avoid the stares of other people? If he died today, none of that mattered. He'd have wasted more than half his life living in fear.

He waited a moment before letting go of Rory's hand, and gave him a smile, hoping Rory got the message that they were okay and that maybe there were things that shouldn't be regretted.

"Thanks." Rory nodded and dusted his hands off on his jeans.

For a few seconds, no one moved or spoke. It was Mike who picked up the shovel and handed it to Jessie. He took it and dropped the first pile of dirt on Rosie. His thought his chest was going to crack open with every breath, but he kept going until Baz took the shovel off him and finished the job. Mike carved her name into the nearby tree with a knife and then it was done.

"What now?" Jessie asked, his voice rough. The plan to drive through the tear had failed.

Rory pressed his lips together and then sighed. "I think we have a lunch. I have a thermos of coffee. We have water and sandwiches."

"How much water? The sea is salt water, right, Jess?" Mike looked at him. "You always said we had to know how much water we had. We need at least two liters per person."

Water and never run off alone were the two things he'd drilled into Mike when he was a small kid visiting for the school holidays. It was easy to get lost, and having water at least gave searchers a chance. "It's cooler here than at home. I have ten in the ute. There's another ten at the bottom of the sea." He glanced at Rory, who nodded. "Four of us, and thirty liters. Do the math, kid. We'll run out of sandwiches first."

"There's steak on legs." Baz hooked his thumb in the direction of the sea and the small herd of cattle.

"That's barely four days of water, and that's assuming we don't use any for cooking," Mike said.

Jessie hadn't expected Mike to do the math quite so fast. "We aren't going to be here four days." They'd have been eaten by then. "We'll spend the rest of today looking for a way back. Home for dinner." His promise sounded hollow, even to himself.

Baz grunted. "And if we aren't, I recommend sleeping on the beach," Baz said. "If the cows think it's safe..."

"Agreed," Rory added. "We can leave it a couple days, then I can take the R22 up and see if I can find a river."

"We could all go up and see if you can find a way through?" Mike sounded just a little too hopeful. The rest of them were well down the path of being stuck here forever. What would some archeologist in the future make of finding a ute and helicopters? "You flew through so maybe the tear is above us?"

"We want to avoid flying, because of the pterosaurs. I'm sure there's a tear at ground level. And we'll find it." How they were supposed to find it Jessie had no idea, though blundering through it had worked the first time. "How many rounds did you bring?" Jessie asked Rory.

"Not enough. A box that's maybe two-thirds full."

"About a dozen in the glove box. What about the emergency gear?" Baz pointed at a locked box on the tray of the ute.

Jessie climbed into the back and flicked open the catches. There wasn't much in there, more first-aid stuff, spare batteries for the radios, water purification tablets, some ration bars, blanket and tarp and rope, and a new box of bullets. He held up the full box of ammo. They were going to have to be careful about how they dealt with dino threats. "No more killing those leggy ones unless we have to, and then we have to take out their partner too."

They sat in the back of the ute and ate sandwiches the way they'd planned to if they'd been busy mustering. That's what they should've done. He should've ignored the lake.

But he knew that he'd have eventually investigated, maybe with Rory who'd have insisted on coming with him. Would they have stumbled through the tear? Or just been left scratching their heads and calling up someone to look at the weird dolphins?

If it were just Rory and him, Baz and Mike and Rosie would've been safe. They would've reported them missing and then a search party would've formed up. Who would miss them now?

He took a small sip of water and nodded at Rory. "What time will your people raise the alarm?"

"Tomorrow night if I don't call in. They'll just assume I'm at your place tonight."

Jessie winced, even though the words hadn't been meant that way. He checked his watch again. Was it worth driving down the trail and hoping for the best?

"You want to try again?" Mike asked.

"Why not, got something better to do today?" He glanced at the somber faces around him, then jumped down and stopped. "Hey, look down the other fork."

Ambling up the trail were three thigh high-armored tanks. He was fairly sure they were herbivores, though it looked like they could do some damage with their tails. The family stopped and glanced at him—no doubt as stunned as he was to be here—then kept going, past the ute and up the trail toward the beach.

"That was amazing." Mike's voice was little more than a whisper.

"Maybe it's not the best idea to hang out on a well-used trail," Rory said.

Jessie had to acknowledge that he had a point.

But if this was where the rip was, he didn't want to be too far away either. He got into the cab and waited for the tap on the roof. The ute crept down the trail, past the fallen tree, and he held his breath waiting for the scenery to change or for his ears to pop. He exhaled. Nothing. Just more trees.

He stopped and checked the fuel gauge. There was a second tank, and it wasn't like they were traveling far. He reversed back up the trail to Rosie's grave and leaned out the window. "Should I try the other fork?"

"Why not?" Baz said.

So he did with exactly the same result. It had to be here somewhere. Desperation clawed at his insides and made his heartbeat quicken.

He backed up again. "What time did we come through?"

"Ten thirty-ish."

"Ten forty-one," Mike said. "That's what the video says. You think it only opens at that time?"

Rory snorted. "Like nature obeys our clocks."

"Maybe it's not nature but a science experiment gone wrong. That's why it wasn't on the news. They don't want people to know," Baz said, like he'd figured out the conspiracy.

Jessie got out of the cab. "Or it moves around, like a living thing."

Rory gave a single nod. "Then how the hell do we hunt and find it?"

CHAPTER 6

The shadows were deepening, and the temperature was dropping, and Jessie was about ready to pack it in for the day. Despite multiple drives down the trail, the portal hadn't opened, nor had they found a tear. Jessie had tried waiting in the spot; they'd tried walking through. Nothing. He'd ventured down the other split in the fork but had seen only more forest.

Now standing waist-deep in ferns and other plants—cold, hungry, and hurting—all Jessie wanted to do was get back to the ute and make camp. But he didn't want to be the one who quit first. Not when Mike still had hope and Rory was acting like they stood a chance.

Baz came and stood next to him. If they went too much further, they'd lose sight of the rope—they'd already run out of that and tied it to a tree. How long until they lost all light and really fucked themselves over? "Seen any sign of the portal?"

"Nothing." Jessie crossed his arms, his gaze on Mike who was up ahead with Rory. They were barely visible and were about to give him a heart attack. He couldn't stand to lose either of them. His heart was still too raw after Rosie. It hurt to breathe every time he expected her to come nosing through the plants to be at his side.

"Do you see that?" Mike pointed at some trees.

Jessie took a few steps forward. "Stay here, so we don't lose the rope."

Baz nodded, rifle held up and ready, but given the noise they were making, Jessie hoped everything with teeth was staying well away. Jessie pushed through, branches whipping at his legs, not wanting to hope that Mike had seen something.

"Yeah." Rory moved even further away.

"What is it?" Jessie called, peering into the forest.

"I thought I saw blue sky." Mike beamed.

Rory stopped and spun. "It was here. Do you see anything, Mike?"

He shook his head. "No. But it was there," he added in a softer voice.

"It's okay, kid. Maybe it was just teasing us." Or maybe it had just been hope.

Rory took a few more steps away; even though he was armed, Jessie wanted to call him back. It was too dangerous.

When he could barely see Rory, Jessie shouted, "We're getting a bit spread out."

Mike and he were unarmed, like sausages left for magpies. He turned and looked back at Baz. He couldn't even see the end of the rope. The ute was completely hidden.

It was several seconds that lasted for an eternity before Rory came stamping back into view, singing an old rock song like that would scare the dinos away. Rory's singing was enough to make dogs howl and ears bleed so maybe it would work.

He rejoined Mike and Jessie. "There was something there, but it rippled away." He started to curse then bit it off. "I think we can assume that it's not static and it won't be sitting here waiting for us."

"That's fucking great." Jessie raked his fingers through his hair.

"At least it's still there," Mike said. "All we have to do is go through before it moves."

Jessie wanted to shake Mike and tell him that they had to survive to do that. He glanced at Rory, but Rory was staring at the place the tear had been.

If it had been there at all, not that he was about to say that out loud. "It's getting dark. We need to get out of the forest and make camp. We can search in the morning."

Mike started wading through the shrubs toward Baz.

Jessie waited for Rory. "Was there really something there?"

"I think so. It was just a glimmer before it vanished."

"Then we got really unlucky."

"Timing is everything." He held Jessie's gaze for a moment too long. "Come on."

They stamped their way back to the ute, then drove to the beach. The cattle were huddled for the night, in the open where they could watch for predators.

But aside from the emu-dino, everything else they'd seen had been either insect, bird or herbivore...at least that's what Mike said and at this point, Mike was the resident expert. Jessie was happy for him to have that distraction.

They made a fire and ate the rest of the sandwiches and finished the lukewarm coffee from Rory's thermos, passing it around in silence. No one was brave enough to put their back to the trees.

"Do you see that?" Rory pointed at something over the water.

Jessie squinted. The sun had almost sunk into the sea, leaving the sky dark and smeared with clouds. "What do you see?"

"That lighter blue patch?" Mike stood.

"I thought it was a cloud," Jessie said. "See the way it moves."

But what if it wasn't a cloud and it was moving because that's what the tear did? Mike turned a little. "If we were over the water, we'd be able to look through and see what's on the other side."

"Home will be on the other side," Baz said.

"Shouldn't it be over the land too? That's how we got through." He searched the sky over the trees, hoping to see the same paler color.

"There," Mike said. "Near the shore."

It took Jessie several seconds of peering and turning his head just so until he could make it out. But it wasn't over land, it was over water.

They were all standing now, staring at what could be anything, all hoping it was the tear. But it seemed to be fading. The blue smear darkening until it blended it with the sky and was gone.

"Do you think it's still there even though we can't see it?" Mike whispered.

"I think we just got two sunsets. Maybe home gets darker later."

Mike snapped his fingers. "Of course. Australia used to be joined to Antarctica and be further south."

Jessie didn't care about continents and their attachments, only how they got home. "That means the best times to see it are first thing in the morning and last thing at night."

Rory pressed his lips together and nodded. "Then we'd best be up early."

But no one was quite ready to sleep. Maybe it was the dinosaurs, or maybe it was seeing the tear for the first time. Jessie was troubled by the way it was only over the water when that morning it had stretched inland. It was moving away from them, and they only had the one R22. Worried gnawed at him. His hand fell to the side, but Rosie wasn't there. He'd caught himself about to whistle for her several times.

Eventually, Mike went to sleep in the cab, as agreed, and Baz set up his swag near the ute, taking one of the rifles with him. That left Rory and him sitting by the fire. Jessie wished he has some rum or bourbon to pour into the hole in his heart Rosie had left. He knew liquor wouldn't fix it, but he'd be able to forget about all of this shit for a while.

If they couldn't catch the tear, how many days until he envied Rosie?

He wanted to put aside four bullets because if one of them got half-eaten, it wouldn't be right to leave them alive and chewed up where no flying doctor was ever going to visit. He fed a twig into the fire and watched the sparks. They were the first humans. The only humans. He almost laughed. Four guys were not going to be an early start to human evolution.

He glanced at Rory's outstretched legs, and let the thought linger, wondering what it would be like. He blamed the heat on his cheeks on the fire but didn't look away. Instead, he let his gaze skim higher until he reached Rory's face.

There was a soft curve on Rory's lips. "What are you thinking about?"

The night closed in around them. The truth was so obvious, but Jessie was a coward. "Getting home."

Rory lifted an eyebrow. "Yeah." He sighed. "Guess I should go up tomorrow and see if I can spot the tear?" Rory asked, glancing up at the sky.

Even that was different somehow. The stars were hung in unfamiliar places. If not for that, and the odd animals calls from the forest, he could almost be sleeping rough on his property. If he was at home, would he be wondering if something might happen? If he should take that risk?

"All of us?" Jessie pulled the blanket tighter around his shoulders and flipped his jeans over. They were taking forever to dry. He'd feel much safer in his own pants. More covered than just in the borrowed T-shirt and shorts. His boots and socks were also by the fire, and it had been bloody nice to get his wet socks off. Rory's blood-stained shirt had been rinsed in the sea and laid to dry by the fire too. All he had was the blanket to hide behind.

If the R22 and Rory went through tomorrow, where did that leave the rest of them? But if Rory made it back to their time, then he could get help...assuming they could find their way back to the past. If the portal was as fickle on their side, as it was in the past, then maybe help wouldn't come. Maybe everything had been bad luck and bad timing.

"I saw what those pterosaurs did to your chopper. If we all cram in..." Rory shook his head.

Jessie nodded. He knew. The R22 would be overweight and wouldn't be able to maneuver as quickly. "And if they come after you anyway?"

Rory's jaw tightened. "What else can I do? We have to keep trying."

"I know... I just..." He glanced at the ute and the swag only a few meters away. Baz and Mike could be awake and listening. "You're my best friend."

And he didn't want to fuck that up just because he had issues, like wanting to invite Rory to come closer to share the warmth of the blanket.

Rory smiled and held Jessie's gaze. Jessie looked away first. His heart was doing that stupid thing where it beat too fast, like there was one of those giant dragonflies caught in his rib cage. Maybe if he'd had half a bottle of rum, he'd be able to say something.

Then Rory moved closer and spoke with a low voice. "Just tell me to fuck off or something, 'cause sometimes when you look at me, I get ideas that I'm not sure you want me having."

"I can't do that." It would be easier if he could. He tossed a twig into the flame and watched it burn. The shame and the subsequent pain when his father had torn strips of him with his belt loomed too large. His father still took up too much space in his head. Last year, at Rory's fortieth, they'd both been drinking, and Jessie had let it slip the reason why Amy had left. If there hadn't have been other people around...now there was no one around. He stared at the flame until his eyeballs started to dry out. "You don't care what everyone else thinks."

"Why do you?"

Why did he? Because real men didn't think about kissing other men. *Because no son of mine...* "I don't want to be the center of gossip. I want to be able to go into town and not have people whisper."

"I go into town. What do people say about me when I'm not there?"

"That it's a shame a nice guy like you hasn't settled down."

Rory laughed. "My mother thinks the same thing. Every time I date someone for more than six months, she gets her hopes up."

"Your parents don't know?"

"Of course they do. And I would like to find the right guy and get married and do all that." A flock of something fluttered through the canopy chirping and carrying on. "Would you marry again?"

"A chick? No." A guy? It was legal and all that, but he didn't want that much fuss. He didn't want people prying and passing judgment. In his head, all the reasons why not were in his father's voice. The snide comments about celebrities, or any guy who didn't conform to his father's narrow ideal. Fuck, even sitting here talking about being gay would've been too much. All the anger his father had carried had eventually blown up inside of him, and he'd had a fatal stroke. Jessie hadn't cried at the funeral, not because it would please his father, but because he didn't give damn. He wanted to step out from the long shadow his father cast and start ignoring the scars on his skin. He pressed his lips together and fed another twig into the crackling fire. "I wouldn't know where to start with a guy."

Rory shrugged. "Same place you always start."

Jessie lifted an eyebrow. "I already have your number."

"See? That was easy. How about I give you a call sometime?"

"Like when we get home?" Jessie frowned. And if they never got home?

"I was thinking sooner." Rory put a hand on Jessie's bare thigh and leaned in close. "Moonlit walk by the ocean where no one will overhear?"

Jessie hesitated, but it was just a walk. It wasn't a date. He stood, keeping hold of the blanket, and Rory picked up the rifle. They made their way to the shore where the waves lapped at the grit that passed for sand. Away from the glow of the fire, the breeze off the water was icy cold, and he shivered. It was definitely the cold, not nerves.

The moonlight glinted off the water. But the water was clear enough that Jessie was sure he could make out the shiny metal of his downed chopper. He watched the water lap at his bare toes, knowing that he'd need to put his boots on in the morning even if they weren't dry.

Rory was close enough that their arms were touching. Jessie's stomach knotted, and he kept his gaze firmly on the water, but he was acutely aware of the man standing next to him. From the sound of his breathing to the way he shifted his weight to be closer. The back of their hands touched. Not since high school, when he'd first started mucking around with a guy and questioning everything, had he been trapped in such a loaded moment.

He uncurled his fingers and let them brush Rory's palm. Rory closed his hand around Jessie's. Jessie held his breath, but the world didn't end. He exhaled and breathed in the salt air. For a few moments, it didn't matter that they were in the wrong time.

After a few more breaths, Jessie found his voice. "Did you want some blanket?"

"Yeah." Rory moved closer and slipped his arm around Jessie's waist so they could share the blanket and watch the sea.

Something splashed in the water and he startled. He searched the surface but whatever it was, was gone. They couldn't stand there all night, but he didn't want to move. He didn't know what they were going to do come daylight.

Nothing was the smart answer. He didn't want Baz and Mike to know.

However, he knew that wasn't being fair to Rory. "Have you been waiting to get me alone?"

"Ever since my birthday, but you always had an excuse."

"Yeah." He was good at that. "I got scared."

"I know...but I figured you'd come around eventually."

"Only took a few million years."

Rory chuckled and turned to face him. "True."

Here they were, a million or so years away from everything. If he couldn't take the chance now, when would he take it? Jessie leaned in closer and put his hand on Rory's stubble-roughened cheek. Rory's breath was warm on his inner wrist. Now he'd made the first move he had to finish it, prove that he could. Before he could wind up the nerve, Rory closed the last few inches and kissed him lightly on the lips.

"We should probably get some rest," Rory murmured, but he didn't move away. His fingers found the hem of the T-shirt and then Jessie's back. His fingers were cool on Jessie's skin as they traced the smooth line of a scar.

He didn't want to answer questions and ruin the night, so he pressed in close and kissed Rory the way he'd wanted to so many times. Rory held him tight and didn't shy away. When they finally pulled apart, Jessie was just a little breathless. They were still too close, and the damn shorts didn't hide a thing. Heat rushed to his face, but in the next heartbeat, he realized that Rory's jeans weren't doing a much better job. Rory's eyes were dark, and his breathing was quick. The last thing Jessie wanted to do was sleep.

A cow bellowed and the herd, that had been sleeping, woke and started moving toward the familiar ute.

Rory whipped his head around. "That can't be a good sign."

The forest went quiet, and the need to run flooded Jessie's veins. They untangled and ran toward the ute. They beat the cattle and climbed into the tray. Rory got the rifle ready, but Jessie hoped he didn't need to use it. The blanket was poor armor.

Something big slunk out of the forest. It was maybe three meters tall, and it stopped where the cattle had been to sniff the shit, before turning its attention to the herd.

Maybe running for the ute, and hiding with the cattle, hadn't been a great idea. Maybe they should've hightailed it up a tree or something.

The dinosaur charged past the campfire that Jessie had been planning to sleep beside and straight toward them. Rory kept it in the rifle sights, but Jessie wasn't sure one bullet would stop it. It was huge and heavier built than the emu-dino. The cattle scattered, but they weren't all quick enough. The beast snatched one up in its jaws and carried the bellowing cow into the forest.

CHAPTER 7

It was several seconds before the captured cow went silent. Jessie remained frozen, staring at the tree line. Rory lowered the rifle with shaking hands. Jessie was glad Rory hadn't shot it—how many bullets would it have taken to kill it, and would he have been quick enough before it got to them?

How long had the cows been here and how many had it eaten? Standing on the beach, they were an easy dinner.

"What was that?" Baz asked next to Jessie.

Jessie nearly jumped out of his skin; he hadn't seen his stockman get up. He drew in a breath. "No fucking idea."

"Nothing good," Rory added. "Maybe staying near the cattle wasn't a smart idea."

"Ya think?" Jessie couldn't keep the sarcasm from his voice. Not that they had many options. "I don't think anywhere here is safe."

The cattle formed up into a herd but stayed close to the ute, like the humans could offer them protection from the dinosaurs.

"What's going on?" Mike stuck his head out the window.

"Nothing, just the cattle getting spooked," Jessie lied.

Baz shook his head and got back into his swag.

Jessie lowered his voice. "I had been planning on sleeping by the fire."

Rory gave him a somber nod. Then smiled. "It's cold in the tray. Better share a blanket."

Jessie wasn't sure he'd get to sleep if Rory were pressed close to him, and he sure as hell didn't want to set the ute rocking. He still wasn't sure about any of this, even though it felt right, like he didn't have to force it and pretend to be someone else. Had Amy felt him trying too hard?

"I'd better get my shoes." He didn't want to lose them. "Spot me."

He slid off the tray. While the stars and fire illuminated the night, Jessie didn't know if he would be fast enough if a dino came out of the trees.

He walked through the cattle, not wanting to spook them, then sprinted the last couple of meters to the fire. He didn't kick sand over it, just swept up the clothes and shoes and socks.

His heartbeat drowned out every sound and he ran back to the ute like his ass was on fire.

"I'm not sure this is any safer," Jessie panted. Especially not now that the cattle had moved in close.

"It's not, but we can pretend it is." Rory put the rifle down between them. "I'll keep first watch?"

"Are you sure? I don't know if I'll be able to sleep anyway."

"I'm sure." Rory leaned over and placed a light kiss on Jessie's cheek that did nothing to calm him. Then he shrugged into his fire-warmed shirt, that Jessie had been wearing only hours ago, and picked up the rifle.

Jessie lay down, expecting to stare at the stars all night with fear and lust coiled tight in his gut. But he must have nodded off because at two, Rory shook him awake and handed him the gun. Jessie wiped the grit from his eyes and sat up. He wanted a drink, but until they found more water, he didn't want to indulge just because he wanted to wet his lips. He thought about taking a leak, but he didn't fancy going over to a tree, or using the back tire. So he waited for dawn and whatever new monster that would bring.

He was sure there were plenty out there. This wasn't a zoo with just one animal on display; this was more like a wildlife safari where everything was dangerous, and they shouldn't be getting out of the car and up close with anything.

Were they changing history by being here?

Maybe they couldn't get back because they'd already done something which meant they'd never been born...but if they hadn't been born, why were they still here? And if they hadn't been born, how could they have changed the past? The thoughts chased around his head. Not enough sleep, not enough coffee, and too much time on his hands.

Usually, there was work to do, if not outside then inside. Paperwork and such.

Now he had nothing.

Rory started snoring, adding to the nighttime noises of the forest. Jessie glanced down and stole a few seconds, then a few minutes. It wouldn't matter if he watched him sleep until daylight. No one else would know.

He made himself more comfortable, loaded rifle in his lap. While his ears listened for silence or unsettled cattle, he watched Rory. Maybe something good could come out of this.

Or maybe they were just trying for something before death caught up with them. He didn't want to be the bitter old guy who only realized that he'd wasted his life too late. While he wasn't old, he certainly wasn't young. If he had more balls, he would've left home at eighteen and gone to live his own life. His whole life had been built on fear.

Fear of his father.

Fear of what people would say.

Fear of himself.

Now he could add fear of dinosaurs to the list.

He'd even kissed Rory out of fear. The fear that he'd never get the chance again.

In the predawn gray, the noises coming from the forest changed and Jessie went on alert. His grip tightened on the rifle, but nothing came out of the forest and the cattle remained calm. He forced himself to relax. But he was still tense and stiff from sitting up and keeping watch. He needed to shake his legs and take a leak.

As quietly as he could, he got off the tray and walked over to the nearest shrub. He pulled the shorts down just enough and stared into the forest, pretending that the weird trees and animal sounds didn't bother him. If anything came at him now, the best he'd be able to do was use the rifle as a club.

Overhead, birds—that didn't look like anything he recognized—flitted about. Not everything here was terrifying. There was a wild green beauty to it...nice for a holiday, not a place he wanted to spend the rest of his life. For a moment, being trapped here alone with Rory didn't seem like a bad option. They could do whatever they wanted and no one would care, but he recognized the fear. Instead of pretending that it didn't exist, he'd acknowledge it was there. And that it wanted to keep him firmly in the closet.

He pulled up the shorts and stood there for a moment longer, hoping that today they got back and one day in the near future—distant future?—they'd look back and if not laugh then at least reminisce. The government would want to know why and how if they weren't behind it. They could tie up his land for years. For all that he wanted things to go back to how they had been, they wouldn't. After last night, they couldn't.

With a final glance at the scrubby undergrowth, he turned his back on the forest and wandered back to the ute. He scanned the sky, looking for a smear of color that didn't belong but didn't see anything.

His gut clenched at the thought that it might have gone overnight.

"See anything?" Mike got out of the cab and leaned on the door. He stretched and then looked over the sea.

"No." Maybe he needed his eyes checked. "You?"

"Maybe, out there." He pointed off into the distance.

"Did you sleep okay?"

Mike rolled his eyes. "As if. I heard the cow get taken."

"I thought you were asleep."

"Like I could sleep through that."

Jessie lifted his eyebrows. Mike had the ability to sleep through several alarms at home.

"I couldn't sleep much. Even though I know you and Rory were up keeping guard." Mike studied his boot and toed at the sand. "I saw you two walk down to the water."

Jessie rocked back on his heels. Mike had seen too much, and Jessie didn't know what to say. He tried to make an excuse or a reason. He needed to say something. "We were looking at the chopper."

Mike smiled like he saw through the lie. "Rory seems into you."

Jessie's heart stopped. If Mike had noticed, had everyone? He was more afraid of what people would say, and think, than dinosaurs. A rifle wouldn't stop the gossip.

"I hadn't noticed. Why would I?" There was an edge in his voice that he didn't like, that reminded him of his father. He wanted to take back the words. He knew Rory liked him and he liked Rory. And he didn't know what to do with it. He'd left it all too late. He was thirty-six, not sixteen.

Mike frowned. "I'm just saying it would be cool...like..." He shrugged. "I don't care. Whatever. Make sure I don't get eaten." He stalked toward the forest.

Jessie watched the trees and let Mike's words tumble around his head until the sharp edges wore away. Mike knew and didn't care. He wanted to take comfort in that, but the scars still ached. They were ugly ridges and a reminder not to step out of line. He wasn't brave...he didn't know what he was, or even who he was. He'd wasted twenty years trying to be what his father expected.

Mike made his way back over. "What's for breakfast?"

Jessie glanced at the cattle.

"Oh. But we won't eat a whole one and won't the carcass attract dinosaurs? I can't believe I just said that." He pushed his fingers through his blue hair, then messed it up like he had somewhere to be. "Can we eat dinosaur?"

"I don't know."

"Could you talk quieter?" Rory sat up. His hair stuck up in all directions.

"We've got to catch and kill breakfast."

"No coffee and toast?"

"Not been invented yet." Mike grinned. "Nothing has been invented. I can make a wheel. Write something. Can I carve my name into trees?"

"Go nuts. There's a bottle opener in the glove box," Jessie said. "Use that instead of the knife."

"Why can't I use the knife?"

"Survival," Jessie said at the same time as Rory said. "We need to keep it sharp."

Mike's gaze flicked between them and for a moment, Jessie thought he was going to say something. With a tilt of his chin, that was so much like Mike's grandfather once he'd made a decision, Mike reached into the glove box and grabbed the bottle opener.

Jessie waited until Mike had wandered off to start his pre-historic graffiti before leaning on the side of the ute to talk to Rory. "How long do you think that will keep him occupied?"

"Not long...you think he's holding up okay?"

"As good as anyone." Jessie shrugged. "He thinks there's something over the water. I can't see shit."

Rory turned and scanned the sky. He squinted. "Yeah, maybe."

"We could try driving around the shore to see if we can get a better angle." But Jessie didn't remember seeing any spits of land.

"I'll go up."

"You should take a shooter with you."

Rory nodded. "Yeah, probably."

They looked at each other, knowing that it wouldn't be Jessie. It would have to be Baz because Mike couldn't shoot.

Jessie sighed. "So do you want cow or dino for breakfast?"

Rory stared at him. "Mike's right, anything we kill will attract scavengers at best."

"So we do it away from here. Or we skip breakfast and try to get back. But if we don't—"

"We'll be tired, hungry and not thinking right," Rory finished.

Jessie glanced over as Baz leaned on the opposite side of the tray. "If you're going to eat dino, you want those armored ones. You don't want scavengers or meat-eaters."

That made sense. Jessie's stomach grumbled. He wanted to eat now, but he wanted to get home more. "How about we try to get back, and we keep an eye out for something small to kill. If we don't see anything, we'll come back and grab a cow."

"If we're still here this afternoon, we need to find out where the cattle are getting their water." Rory scratched at his jaw.

Jessie had a sick feeling that they would still be here. By tonight, Rory's stockman would be concerned, and he'd make some calls and arrange something. No doubt he'd see the lake and the not-dolphins and wonder what the hell was going on. Hopefully, he wouldn't accidentally come through.

"So what's the plan? More driving around?" Baz asked.

That was their only plan. They were hoping to find the tear and go through.

"I'll prep the R22." Rory got up, had a drink, and made his way to the chopper.

"He's going up alone?" Baz asked.

"I was thinking you should go with him, to shoot anything that comes close."

Baz kicked the sand. "Aw fuck, you know I hate going up in those things."

"Strap in, take a rifle, and make sure the pterosaurs don't take him down."

"You go, I'll stay with Mike. Or better yet, send Mike."

Jessie scanned the sea, but if they were out there, they were too far away to see. Maybe they were farther up the coast and he'd just gotten unlucky. "I thought about it. If Rory gets through, then Mike's clear. But you're a better shot than him and he's my nephew. Go with Rory, please."

"Do you think he'll make it back home?"

Jessie wanted to nod but couldn't. "Even if he doesn't, his people will raise the alarm."

"Which is all well and good if the portal still exists." Baz fixed him with a look. "You think we're stuck here."

"Well, I'm not holding my breath...just trying to keep positive for Mike."

"No place for a kid. We've at least lived." Baz grinned and wandered over to the chopper.

While Jessie had lived, he wasn't sure he'd ever truly been alive. Last night, he'd tasted it for just a moment. Too little too late.

Rory started the chopper, gave him the thumbs up, and lifted off in a swish of sand. For several heartbeats, Jessie watched, his heart pumping hard, and his gut twisting. But the sky remained clear.

The chopper swept over head then cruised over the top of the trees like Rory was searching for a lost calf. He swept toward the coast and back toward the trail, then repeated the process. Jessie watched him methodically cover every inch.

He took his eyes off Rory and Baz to check on Mike. Mike was carving all their names into a tree. Jessie took a moment to shuck the shorts and pull his jeans on. When he looked up to the sky to locate the R22 this time, it was farther over the water. Jessie tensed but Rory turned and skimmed the trees. Jessie kept waiting for the chopper to keep flying and disappear into the future. It didn't. Rory widened his search, each time heading farther over the sea.

Jessie scanned the horizon. North, or what he thought of as north, there were birds in the sky. He opened the cab door and pulled out the radio. "Rory, you there?"

"Yeah."

"There's pterosaurs behind you."

The R22 turned and Baz put his rifle out the side.

"I see them. I think there's something over the sea. Your lake, that had to come from somewhere. What if the constant bleed is over the water?"

"How far out?"

"Hard to estimate."

Jessie watched the pterosaurs get closer, their large wings making them faster than should be possible. His heart clenched like a fist and he couldn't breathe. He wanted Rory to get home, but the pterosaurs were closing in too fast. "They'll be on you fast, your call."

If their only way out was over the water and Rory left them, they were screwed until help came. If it came. Rory turned and came toward the shore fast. "I'm coming back."

Baz fired a couple of shots that startled the pterosaurs, buying Rory the extra seconds he needed. Rory's skids kissed the top of the waves before he landed about a hundred meters south.

The pterosaurs swooped in close to the shore before wheeling away now that the threat was gone. Their wingspan was bigger than Jessie was tall. There was a grace to them that made him think of the fighter pilots at the air show he'd been to once when at school. They flew close and tight when preparing to attack but as they flew away, they spread out, flying in a formation only they knew.

Baz almost jumped out of the chopper.

Rory followed more slowly, watching the pterosaurs as he walked. "That was a little close. They move a bit too damn quickly for my liking."

"They clearly don't like other flying things in their territory." With everyone back on the ground, he sat in the tray and pulled on his socks and boots. The boots were pretty dry, which made for a nice change.

"That's unfortunate for us. I think the bleed's out there," Rory said.

"Did you see it for sure?" Jessie glanced at Rory and then Baz.

Baz shook his head. "I was watching for those damn dinos."

"I thought I saw dry land."

"But?"

"But that far out, there's bigger things than dino-dolphins. The water's clear enough that I could almost see to the bottom. Whatever it is, is the size of a whale. And if they," he pointed at the specks that remained of the pterosaurs, "bring us down, we're dinner."

CHAPTER 8

Jessie sipped his ration of water and leaned on the edge of the tray. He was well sick of searching for the elusive tear on land. It had been here and now it had moved. Nothing resembling lunch had ambled past, probably because they were making too much noise driving back and forth and exploring all the trails. Even at the magical hour of 10:41, there was nothing to be seen. That had hit Mike the hardest.

Now he sat sullenly on the front seat.

Rory had said nothing about his find and neither had Jessie. If Rory was wrong about what he'd seen, then it was a bloody big risk to take. They might not live to regret it. But for how long did they wait and hope that either help would come, or that the tear would appear in front of them?

"I don't know about you lot, but I'm hungry. I think it's time to make lunch and consider our options," Baz said, like they had options.

"We're stuck here forever, aren't we?" Mike got out of the car and slammed the door. He stomped two meters away and swore loudly at the top of his lungs, startling several birds into a squawking frenzy. He kicked at a fern, snapping it off at the stem, then turned back to the ute. "We're all fucking dead."

If Jessie had been a few years younger, he'd have joined in with the hopeless tantrum. No one stopped Mike or told him to calm down. Mike swept his hair off his face and glared at the adults.

"My stockman will raise the alarm this afternoon," Rory said, like that was the solution.

Mike turned on him. "You're assuming there's still a tear. That time is still moving the same. What if no time has passed? What if the portal only works between fixed points in time? Or what if it jumps around and the rescue part it a million years too early or—"

"You've put far too much thought into this, Mike. I don't know the answer, but I want to get home as much as you." Jessie grabbed his nephew's shirt. "Yelling at us isn't going to help, okay?"

Mike broke free and for a moment looked as though he was going to take a swing; instead, he drew in a breath. His fingers were still curled into fists and his mouth was a thin line. For a second, Jessie saw the echo of his father in Mike's anger. He stepped back.

It was enough for Mike to get control. "I just want to go home. I know I've fucked things up with Dad. And I don't want to die without fixing it."

"Your Dad's worried, that's all. He didn't send you to me as punishment, but because you always like the place and he hoped that you'd be able to find yourself again." Jessie didn't add that he knew about the dabbling in drugs and getting expelled.

"Well, that was a fail, wasn't it? Now I'm more lost than ever." Mike sighed. "Guess I should apologize."

"Nah, kid, you just said what we're all thinking but didn't have the balls to say," Baz said.

Rory laughed, breaking the tension. "I think we all need something to eat. I hear the first ever beachside steak house is opening up. We should try it." He caught Jessie's gaze and the smile vanished.

They couldn't spend their days waiting for the tear to come back this way. What if it drifted farther out to sea? If they were wrong, if they didn't make it back home through the tear, they'd never survive the swim back to shore.

Jessie nodded. "Let's catch and kill lunch." There was no way those cows were making their way back home, and they were only going to get eaten by dinosaurs anyway.

They rode back to the beach, Jessie and Rory in the back, and followed the tracks in the sand to the herd. The cattle had moved north up the coast, to where a stream trickled out to sea. They could eat lunch here, leaving the carcass far from camp. The cattle were sticking close together, like they knew that something had gone horribly wrong, but the food was tasty, so it wasn't all bad. Still, their ears flicked, and they gave the ute and humans a wary glance as they edged away.

"You want me to do it?" Rory lifted his rifle slightly.

"No. It's going to be a waste though. Half a ton of cow, and we'll be lucky to eat a kilo."

"Speak for yourself. I'm starving." He lowered his voice and leaned in. "And if we aren't going to try flying out, we should keep some for tomorrow."

"I don't know what we should do. It feels like everything is the wrong choice."

"Everything?" The smile was gone from Rory's voice.

Jessie put a hand on Rory's thigh. "Maybe not everything. That one on the left, on her own." She was a bit smaller than the others. Maybe she'd be nice and tender. It wasn't like they had salt or sauce or sides to serve with the meat.

He got out of the ute and took his time to get the shot right. Then dinner dropped to its knees. They waited for the other cattle to realize and pay their respects. Then Rory and Jessie made quick work of getting what they needed for a very late lunch while Baz stood guard.

"You've got some interest," Baz said

"Yeah, we're getting there," Jessie said. But the knives he had weren't made for butchering and cow hide was tough. He glanced over the stream to where some of the small chicken-like dinos watched. The longer he watched, the more gathered, waiting for their chance at the carcass. Leaving so much meat was a waste, but they had no way of storing it and, honestly, keeping this much meat nearby was a risk they couldn't afford to take. Jessie jerked his chin at the dinos. "I don't think they ever sleep."

Rory glanced over his shoulder. "It won't be long until the bigger ones show up."

"There must be herbivores about...things they naturally eat."

"Yeah, but they're better at running and hiding than the cattle."

"True." And when the cattle ran out, they'd have to hunt dinos. If they were still here...

"This is the worst butchering job I've ever done." Rory cut through the last of the tendons holding the leg on. They weren't going for neat cuts, but ease of cutting and carrying. If it had been up to Jessie, some slow-cooked ribs would've been nice or a bit of ribeye steak. But they'd barely had time to take a leg, and no time to prepare the meat properly.

"What do you think about the tear? We drove through easily, and there were ferns on my land. It had to have been there for a while."

"Yeah, I've been thinking about it, even before Mike's outburst. What if it's getting smaller?"

"I was worried that it might be moving, heading farther out to sea."

Rory nodded. "Either way, if we don't act soon, we're fucked." He smiled. "Of course, I could be wrong. And it's flickering all over the place and we just have to be patient."

"Get eaten on land, get eaten in the water... If it were just you and me, what would you do?" Jessie wiped his bloodied knife clean on a fern. He'd wash it properly when they were away from the carcass and the meat was cooking.

Rory considered him for several seconds, his lips curved. "First, I'd make sure there were no regrets, and nothing left unsaid or undone. Then I'd fly over that sea like every monster that lives here was chasing me."

"And if there's no tear when you get there?" He spread out the tarp and Rory dropped the cow leg onto it.

Rory was silent for several seconds as he folded the tarp around the leg. "Then I guess I try to fly back to land and we live as best as we can for as long as we can. But it's not just you and me and I reckon Baz and Mike get a say."

They'd barely gotten into the ute with their dinner, before the little scavengers swarmed the carcass en masse. There were at least fifteen of them, screeching and jostling for the best bits. Jessie resisted the urge to shoo them away, but only just. He was glad he'd buried Rosie deep, but knew that if they died, they wouldn't be so lucky.

He rapped on the roof and Baz drove the ute about thirty meters away. It felt too close, but no one wanted to be cooking meat where they planned to sleep. Nor did they want to be finding somewhere else to make camp, because that would be admitting they were never getting home. This was temporary.

"Why do you think it formed?" Jessie helped heft the leg out of the tray.

Rory shrugged. "I'm leaving that to the scientists and government suits."

They made a fire and cut the meat up into smaller pieces so that it would cook faster. Rory used one of the metal drinking cups to boil off some sea water and get salt and their late lunch was enough to fill their stomachs and lift their spirits. But they all kept an eye on the scavengers as they fed.

They all watched the tree line and listened for the arrival of something bigger.

The cold breeze off the sea kicked up and the temperature started to drop as the sun started to inch its way down to the sea. The knowledge that they'd be spending another night here was almost too much.

"I got some footage of the little ones," Mike said. "But even with the power pack, my phone won't last much longer. I think if we can't get back, I should put it in a Ziploc bag. Make a time capsule. Maybe someone will find it and figure out what happened. We're stuck here, aren't we?"

"We're trying'" Jessie said.

"I'm not a kid, so don't lie."

Baz stood. "I'm going to water a tree."

Jessie sighed. Baz didn't want to be caught in family arguments and Jessie didn't blame him. If they got back, Baz was getting a bonus.

"I thought I saw something over the sea, but I didn't get close enough. We think," Rory paused to glance at Jessie, "it's either moving or shrinking."

"But we'd have to fly over the sea?" Mike gave each of them a look. "Where the *Kronosaurus* lives. You know, from the museums? Like a giant shark."

Jessie shook his head. He'd never been into dinosaurs. "You mentioned that one before."

"Because it's kind of famous and huge."

"That must be the big thing I saw." Rory frowned.

"Yeah, it's the size of a bus and eats everything smaller than it. So if the pterosaurs attack, or something happens and we're out over the sea—"

"That might be the only way home," Jessie said before Mike could wind up again.

Mike blinked, his mouth hanging open. "Fuck. Those baby choppers aren't made for four."

"We'll be flying low and as fast as we can. I have enough fuel to make one run at it and still get us back to land if there's nothing." Rory's gaze scanned the tree line.

Baz was making his way back, rifle in his hand, gaze on the scavengers.

"Have a think. We'll talk to Baz then take a vote." Jessie stood, ready to follow in Baz's footsteps. Jessie barely saw the dark green shadow move, then two of the emu-dinos tore out of the shrubs toward Baz. "Run!"

But it didn't matter how fast Baz ran, the dinos were faster. They sprinted like an emu. Baz dropped the rifle and pumped his arms and legs. Fear stretched his eyes wide.

Rory fired; sand kicked up behind the dino, but it didn't stop. Baz changed direction, hoping to throw them off, but they pivoted just as fast. One cut in front. The other leaped on Baz's back. He went down.

Rory fired again and hit the dino in the side. It turned and hissed and for a heartbeat, Jessie was frozen. Some part of his brain remembered what it was like to be prey and he couldn't think how best to escape.

Mike grabbed his hand. "Get in the car."

It was enough to snap him out of his daze. Baz screamed.

Rory was still kneeling, rifle ready. "If I kill one, I have to kill both. I don't know if I'll be fast enough."

Baz screamed as the dinos tore him apart.

Baz was already dead; he just didn't know it. "You only need one shot."

Rory glanced up at Jessie, then closed his eyes as he understood. "Shit."

"Get in the car, Uncle Jess." Mike had the door open.

Rory's hand shook as he sighed down the barrel. "I can't get a clean shot."

Jessie glanced between Rory, Mike, and Baz. "Get in the ute. I'll drive us closer."

Rory scrambled up and in. The three of them were squeezed into the front seat like sardines. Mike in the middle, Jessie driving, and Rory with the rifle sticking out the window like they were pretending the ute was a dino-proof tank.

Jessie spun the ute, knowing this wasn't a rescue. They couldn't save Baz. Even if they'd had a fully equipped hospital, he wasn't sure that anything could be done. Then the screams stopped and became a guttural gurgle.

And that was worse.

"He's dying," Mike's voice hitched.

Jessie got as close as he dared and slowed. Rory took a shot and Baz went quiet. Both dinos lifted their heads and glared at the ute, as if they preferred their meals alive. Jessie took that as his cue to fuck off fast.

CHAPTER 9

Jessie checked the rearview mirror. The emu-dinos that had attacked Baz were giving chase. "Put your window up."

Rory pulled the rifle in and wound up the window. Jessie did the same. Then he followed the shoreline, past where they'd made camp the previous night, hoping that by some miracle the tear in time would be in front of them and they'd be able to drive through.

The ute rocked, as one of the dinos jumped into the back. Jessie swerved, trying to throw it out. It fell over with a thump.

Something crashed into the side of the ute. Rory swore. The rifle slammed into Jessie's wounded arm and he grunted. He wrapped the steering wheel hard, spinning the ute and spraying sand everywhere, determined to run the bastards over. The one in the tray skidded around, unable to stand up, but it was still there.

The glass behind them broke. A clawed foot poked through. Mike yelped and ducked, almost folding in half. Rory used the rifle as a club, slamming it into the dino's toes. The dino bellowed. Jessie wasn't sure who was more shocked the people or the dinosaur. It pulled its foot free, then tried to shove its head through the hole, snapping and snarling far too close to Jessie's ear. The stink of meat and unbrushed teeth filled the cab.

That wasn't just any meat. It was Baz's blood and flesh.

Jessie's stomach heaved but he swallowed and yanked the car hard, wanting thing out of his tray—but also wanting to avoid rolling the ute which would make them gift wrapped prey. Its partner headbutted Jessie's door. Jessie wasn't wasting time dancing with it. He turned into it and ran it down. The ute bounced over the dino with a sickening crunch.

"Is it dead?" Mike whispered.

Probably not. But Jessie kept that to himself. He hated leaving animals in pain, even if they were trying to kill him.

"Cover your ears." Rory had turned around. He had the rifle over Mike's back and when the dino stuck its snout in through the broken glass, Rory fired twice. Blood and brains and bone exploded. "Go back to the other one."

Jessie didn't argue. He peered through the bloodied windscreen and scraped aside brain matter with the side of his hand, which didn't improve visibility at all. The other emu-dino was still alive but couldn't get up. One of its long legs was broken. He pulled up alongside and Rory got out and killed it with one shot. It was more mercy than it had shown Baz.

For several seconds, no one said anything. Jessie unclenched his hands from around the steering wheel. His knuckles ached from gripping too tight and he was sure a heart attack was just around the corner. His car was going to stink and attract scavengers and predators from a mile away. "Is everyone okay?"

"I think so." Mike cautiously sat up. He wiped the back of his neck and his hand came away bloody. "I'm pretty sure it's not mine."

Rory got back into the cab, sighed, and closed his eyes. "I'm fine."

He didn't look fine. There was no smile on his lips and his breathing was little more than pants. "Where's the other gun?"

"Baz had it," Mike said softly, like he was about to break. Jessie wouldn't have held it against him if he'd started crying, but Mike pulled it together.

"Right." But Jessie made no effort to drive back toward Baz. They needed the weapon though. "I guess we have to go get it?"

"Yeah." Rory nodded.

Jessie headed back to where they'd come from. The scavengers were still all over the carcass, but some had relocated and were all over Baz. Plucking at his flesh like he was just another pile of meat. He put his hand on the horn, but Rory reached over and stopped him before he could press it.

"We can't let them—"

"We can't stop them." Rory's grip tightened around his hand. "We need to focus on living."

Jessie stared at him, knowing he was right, but not wanting nature to do its thing and devour Baz. "We need to do something."

"There's over thirty of the little monsters...that's not good odds and a waste of ammo."

Jessie closed his eyes, then gave Rory's hand a squeeze. He didn't like it, but he could accept it. Baz was dead. At least he wasn't hurting.

"Can you have your moment later, like when we're home?" Mike said.

Rory released Jessie's hand and leaned back. "Can you see the rifle?"

They all peered out the windows.

Jessie crept around the swarm of scavengers, trying not to think about what they were eating. He knew that even if he shooed them away, they'd return as soon as he turned his back. "We should bury him."

"Or we can go," Rory said.

"You mean fly over the sea?" Mike's voice caught. "You don't think we should wait another day? Wait until morning? The sun's setting..."

Jessie glanced over his nephew's head at Rory. Would waiting another night matter, or would the delay cost them their chance?

"We have an hour of daylight, more than enough time to make the flight," Rory said without breaking eye contact with Jessie. "But I want to be very clear, that there's a damn good chance we won't make it if the pterosaurs attack. The hole may have moved or vanished—"

"Why didn't you just go through and get help?" Mike asked.

Jessie knew from the way Rory looked at him; he should've never admitted that he liked him. Then Rory would've gone, and at least he and Baz would've been safe.

"Because I couldn't leave you all behind." Rory looked away. "And I got scared. What if I went through and it closed?

As it was, I barely made it back to the beach. It's a one-shot thing."

"If it's shrinking or drifting out to sea, we should go tonight when the tear is most visible."

Mike chewed his lip. "We're going to die, aren't we?"

Jessie didn't want to agree, but the chances were high that they wouldn't make it, but it was better than sitting around waiting to be eaten. Wasn't it? They might get a few more days. But he wanted a chance at more. He just figured out what he wanted and how to break free of his father's hatred.

"And if we sit here, we die too," Rory said. "I see the rifle."

Jessie steered to where Rory pointed. The scavengers watched but didn't run away from the kill. "Be careful."

"Always." Rory flashed him a grin. Then got out of the cab and walked calmly toward the rifle. It was only a meter away, but the scavengers were just as close. They squawked as Rory got near and a few leaped toward him as if they were going to attack. Rory jumped and threw his arms wide. "Boo!"

The little dinos scattered and Rory got back in the cab. "Let's get out of here."

Jessie drove down the beach to where the R22 waited, then parked. "So are we doing this?"

Rory nodded.

Mike pressed his lips together. "I don't want to get eaten. If I survive this, I'm going to be in therapy for years." He closed his eyes. "I really wanted someone to rescue us."

"That's not what happens. Most of the time, you have to get yourself in a position to be rescued. Give yourself the best chance of survival," Jessie said. He knew the risks when he went out to the edges of his property. He planned accordingly. "We still have a sat phone, and when we get back, we can call for help. But we have to get back. And we can't do it on the ground. But if you don't want to, I'll stay with you and Rory can go back...forward...whatever." He was sick of trying to figure out time travel.

The cab was quiet. The engine ticked as it cooled.

Mike shook his head. "No, we should all go."

"Okay. Why don't you make your time capsule? If we don't make it, maybe someone will find it in the future." Rory got out of the cab and walked over the waiting chopper.

Jessie watched as he started walking 'round the R22, making the preliminary checks. Then he turned his attention to Mike. "Are you really okay with this?"

"I want to go home...if you think this is the only way, then that's it. It's doesn't really matter how I feel."

"None of us like it. But if we don't take this chance..."

"Then we could be stuck, and we'll get eaten anyway." Mike nodded. "Go and help him. I'll write a letter and make the capsule and stay in the ute like a kid who can't be trusted not to run off and play with the dinosaurs."

Seven years ago, that might have been true, but not anymore. Jessie leaned over and kissed the top of Mike's blue hair. "I don't want you running around like bait."

"Trust me, that is not going to happen. But can I go through your toolbox in the back?"

"Yeah. Whatever is there, you can use. We won't be taking any of it back." Jessie got out of the ute, but left the door open for Mike.

"We're bringing the time capsule with us, right? Because I don't want to leave my phone behind if we make it."

"Don't make it too big." He didn't want any extra weight in the chopper.

Rory was obviously thinking the same thing because he was tossing things from the back onto the sand.

"We probably shouldn't be littering."

"We probably shouldn't be here. We could go back and find the whole world changed."

Jessie's world already was. "I can think of a few things I'd like to change."

Rory stuck his head out of the cockpit to look at Jessie. "Yeah? Like what?"

"You know."

"I want to hear you say it, so I can hold you to it later."

"You really think there'll be a later?" Jessie scuffed his boot in the sand. It was easy to be brave and imagine himself living a different life when death was almost assured. But the old fears were still there.

"I'm not ready to abandon all hope. I've waited a bloody long time for you to do more than look."

"Why didn't you do something sooner if you knew?"

"Because you'd have bolted and run, and I still wanted you as a friend." He smiled. "Still do."

"I don't want to lose you as a friend either...so if this doesn't work..." How could it ever work? It was a dream given life by desperation.

Rory jumped down and pressed Jessie against the warm metal of the chopper. One hand landed next to Jessie's head, then he kissed him hard and hungry. He drew back. "I'll be bloody disappointed if we die before I get you naked."

Jessie's lips ached and he wanted more. If they'd been alone, then maybe he'd have gotten naked for a first and last fuck with Rory. "I wouldn't know what to do anyway."

"So? I do." The grin was back. "I can't believe I almost want one more night here." He rested his forehead on Jessie's. "Almost."

"Same." The word fell off his tongue before he could hold it back. He wanted to know what he'd been running away from his whole life.

"Really?"

"Yeah." It wasn't like he had anything left to lose. He might be dead inside the hour. "When we get back, don't let me run away. I don't want things to go back to how they were."

"I can't drag you out. You have to do that on your own."

"At least hold my hand."

"That I can do." Rory grabbed Jessie's hand. "I won't let go."

CHAPTER 10

"I'll sit in the back. There's no seat, or harness, and if we pitch into the sea, I'll have a better chance of getting out," Jessie said. He didn't want Mike to drown while trapped in the back. Although if they did end up in the sea, would drowning be better than being eaten?

Every time he closed his eyes, he saw Baz. Heard his screams. And knew it could have easily been any one of them. For how long had those things been watching and waiting, hiding in the shadows while they had happily pissed on a tree thinking they were safe?

"I'm thinner and can squeeze through the gap between the seats easier. Besides, you're a better shot." Mike brushed past him and jumped into the back of the R22 before Jessie could argue.

"He's got point," Rory said as he put his headset on. The blades started to whirr.

Jessie touched his shirt pocket, which held an extra three rounds. Both rifles were fully loaded. But every shot had to count. He prayed he didn't need to make any. They'd fly out, find the tear, go through, and celebrate being home. Easy. He kept playing that thought through his mind in the hope that if he believed hard enough, it would come true. Jessie climbed in and took his place next to Rory.

Rory turned to Mike. "Don't shoot me and don't shoot up. If you ping a blade, we're well and truly fucked."

"Got it." Mike gave the thumbs up too.

Jessie put on the spare headset and adjusted the mic. "I guess we're ready."

Rory nodded, then reached over and clasped Jessie's hand. "We can do this."

Jessie didn't know if Rory was referring to the flight or what happened after. His heart hammered under his ribs, and his stomach rocked uneasily as the chopper lifted off. Usually, he loved flying. He glanced back at Mike, already in position with the rifle angled down protecting Rory, then Jessie turned as far as he could in the harness so he could watch the other side. Below his feet the sand vanished, and they were over the water.

Rory took them as high as the tree line then pushed the R22 as fast as it would go. The waves bounced below them in a blur, and the icy wind tugged at Jessie's T-shirt. He was sure he felt salt spray on his face, but he kept his gaze on the sky, not the water. He didn't want to look down and see what was below.

Dino-dolphins, just like at home. That was all. Turtles too, according to Mike.

"See that odd patch of sky...that's where we're heading." Rory's voice was in his ear, tinny from the headset.

Jessie risked a few seconds to follow where Rory was pointing. The area of sky was a vertical sliver of blue, among another wise pretty pink sunset. The sun was still fully up, not even kissing the water. "Has it moved?"

"No, but I swear it was wider this morning."

Jessie snapped his gaze back to the sky behind them. It was still clear. There was some movement farther south, but the pterosaurs were specks against the coast.

Mike tapped his elbow and Jessie turned. Then Mike pointed down.

Jessie didn't need to look past Rory to see what Mike was pointing to. Below them was a massive dark shape, and it was keeping pace. The water was suddenly far too close. Was the thing—and it had to be the *Kronosaurus*—tracking them?

Hunting them.

"Below, Rory."

"I see it." He took them up a little, but otherwise kept his gaze on the sliver of blue that didn't belong.

Jessie scanned the sky again. The specks were bigger. "Fuck."

"Can you be a bit more specific?" Rory asked.

"Pterosaurs on my side." When he glanced down, he was sure the monster was closer to the surface, just cruising along beneath them as though it was a game. The chopper's shadow floated next to the beast.

"We're almost there."

Jessie wasn't so sure. It looked like the blue was still the same distance away. He glanced at the fuel gauge, but there was still enough to get them back to shore just like Rory had said. Not that they'd ever reach dry land. The pterosaurs would make sure of that. They'd have to keep flying if the blue turned out to be nothing. How big was this sea?

The pterosaurs were close enough now that he could clearly see they weren't birds. Their enormous wingspan gave them impossible speed. The shadow beneath them dropped away and Jessie exhaled, glad one dinosaur didn't want to eat them but didn't ease his grip on the rifle.

The pterosaurs broke pursuit and wheeled up, hopefully heading home. His lips twitched into a smile, then his gut

tightened. If the dino-birds were getting the fuck out of here...
"Take us up, now."

Rory didn't hesitate. The R22 jerked up.

Jessie searched the sea. For several heartbeats, he saw
nothing but water. Then a small patch darkened, and the
darkness grew.

"Higher." He readied the rifle, but it was going to be like
throwing peas at a cow.

The *Kronosaurus* broke the surface like a breaching whale.
It lifted out of the water, all open mouth and teeth beneath
them. Jessie stared into its open maw and a wave of dizziness
made him feel like he was falling into its jaws. Then the
beast's mouth snapped closed and it sunk beneath the waves.

It was several rapid heartbeats before Jessie found his
voice. His gaze still locked on the water below. It hadn't
gotten close. But at the same time, it had been far too close.
"Did you see that?"

"I wish I hadn't," Rory said.

The rim of the sun touched the sea. They'd lose light fast
now. The glimmer of blue was definitely closer though.

"No second thoughts—through the portal, or tear, or
whatever you want to call it, even if it's not home?" Rory's
voice was tight, and his gaze now flicked between the water
and the blue.

They hadn't discussed what would happen if it wasn't home on the other side. But what other choice was there?

"Yes." He turned to look at Mike and gave him smile, like everything was great. Then pointed out the front at the window out of here. Hopefully, they didn't up even further in the past.

Rory flew straight at the darkening streak of blue. When the sun set at home, they'd lose the tear in the dark. As they got closer, the tear appeared more like a smear about a hundred meters across.

"It's smaller and farther out to sea today."

"I'm glad we didn't wait." There might have been nothing for them to find in the morning.

"I'm going to have to drop us down to go through." Even through the headset, Rory's voice was tight.

That was when Jessie noticed the tear didn't go up forever. The top was lower than they were flying. He searched the water, now dark to match the sky. It would be impossible to see the rising monster until it was out of the water.

"Just get us through. I trust you." He smiled at Rory.

Rory nodded, no happy grin on his lips. Their lives were in his hands.

It was hard to judge distance over open dark water, but they were closing in on the portal. It widened before them and on the other side, all Jessie could see was more water. For a moment, his gut lurched, but then he remembered the lake. That's all he was seeing.

They'd be fine.

And if he was wrong, and it was somewhere else—an endless ocean? They had maybe another hour of flying and then they'd be out of fuel. They were done. He closed his eyes and drew in a breath. This had to be okay. But his guts churned.

"Flying through was a little rough last time, so it's likely to be the same," Rory said.

Jessie turned and tapped Mike's knee. Mike pulled the gun in and curled up in the back, with his hands over his head as they'd discussed. He was a good kid.

"Approaching the tear," Rory announced like he was landing a 747 on a difficult runway. "And we're going through in three, two...one and a half...one."

A movement beneath Jessie's feet made him glance down. The water erupted at the base of the tear.

His ears popped as they went through. The chopper rocked and lost altitude like it had hit a pocket of air. The water before him shimmered gold in the afternoon sun, and the bank of the lake was clearly visible, brown and green and dotted with cows. His land. His heart swelled and he could've cried with relief.

"I think we're home." He couldn't stop the grin.

Something slammed into the underside of the chopper and almost knocked them out of the sky. Rory battled for control, but they were being dragged down.

Jessie twisted in his seat and peered out the side, trying to work out what had happened.

They were through, but so was the *Kronosaurus*.

CHAPTER 11

The *Kronosaurus* was latched on to the chopper's skids and as it fell toward the water, it was taking them with it. If it dragged them back through the tear, they were dead.

"I can't break free." The engine whined as Rory struggled to get control of the R22.

"It has us. We're going to hit the water," Jessie said. The best they could hope for was staying on the right side of time.

The front of the R22 slammed into the saltwater lake. The windscreen split. Jessie exhaled. He was getting his money's worth out of the helicopter crash course he'd done. He'd never expected to use the information about water escapes, but he was glad he'd paid attention. Water swirled about his ankles. He took off the headset. Whatever happened they had to get out. They were going to have to swim.

The lake wasn't that big, but it was full of ichthyosaurs.

And he wasn't a fast swimmer.

The chopper shuddered and crumpled around him. Mike screamed.

Massive teeth poked through the metal. The *Kronosaurus* was going to crush it like a soft drink can with them still inside. He grabbed Mike's arm to get him moving. "We've got to go."

Maybe the *Kronosaurus* wouldn't notice they weren't in the chopper anymore. The dinosaur wouldn't even know what a helicopter was.

Rory unclipped his harness. Beyond Rory, all Jessie could see was the tongue and mouth of the dinosaur. "Go, I'll be right behind you."

"Dive, to clear the blades." He pointed forward, away from the tear and toward the closest bank. The one they'd stood on only yesterday and wondered where the water had come from. Jessie undid the harness, took a last breath of air, and dove into the cold salt water.

Once in the water, he slung the rifle over his shoulder to free up his hands and he kicked as fast as he could to clear the area for Mike and Rory to escape. The lake didn't seem that deep now that he was in it. But he wasn't about to stop and take a closer look. He kept going until his lungs hurt. Then he surfaced and looked behind. The R22's tail was up in the air.

He couldn't see the *Kronosaurus*. Waves, caused by the thrashing of the oversized dinosaur, slapped into his chest and face. Blood stained the water. Human? Or had the dinosaur cut its mouth on the chopper blades?

Mike broke the surface a few meters away. "We need to get to shore. There's ichthyosaurs in here, and they eat meat."

Of course they did.

"Where's Rory?"

"He was behind me." Mike smoothly swam over. "Come on. We need to get out of here."

Mike was right, but Jessie didn't want to leave Rory in the dino-infested lake. Mike turned to go without him. Jessie saw the fins in the water, heading toward the chopper and the blood. He needed to get clear of the bloodied water.

"Rory!" he shouted as he trod water trying to see him, but there was too much movement.

Something bumped his leg and the animal part of his brain kicked in. He swam after Mike, sure he was about to be dinner.

After only a few strokes, something nudged his boot. He almost died on the spot but when it happened again, he realized it was the bottom of the lake. He could stand. So he did, chest deep in the lake. He waded after Mike who was splashing toward the shore.

When the water only lapped at his waist, Jessie turned around to face the wreck.

The ichthyosaurs were still hunting, and they were close to the chopper and where the *Kronosaurus* still struggled, trapped by the too shallow water. That was almost too good to be true.

"Rory!" Jessie yelled.

Had he drowned? Been eaten? A hundred different scenarios rattled through his head, none of them good. He should've waited. Rory might be hurt or trapped.

The *Kronosaurus* tossed its head and the R22 came free, arcing through the air to land it the lake halfway between Jessie and the beast. The broken chopper lurched then settled upside down, the under belly and skids out of the water. Rory surfaced just in front of the chopper. The instant relief that had bloomed froze in Jessie's chest. Behind him were three fins as the ichthyosaurs stalked him.

"Hurry up." He didn't want Rory wasting time looking behind.

Jessie unslung the rifle. Everything was wet, but he was sure it would still fire; if it didn't, he'd use it as a club. He waded a few steps forward, then stopped. It would do no good if he were attacked as well.

He aimed just below the fin and fired twice, then again at another one, giving Rory a chance.

A few more meters and Rory would be able to stand. How much depth did the ichthyosaurs need to swim? Was he safe? Jessie glanced down, but there was nothing swimming around his legs.

Rory went under and the water churned. Jessie's breath caught. Then Rory resurfaced, and Jessie didn't hesitate this time. He plowed through the water, desperate to reach him. He couldn't lose the man he'd never let himself love. They deserved a chance. Rory changed direction and headed for the much closer chopper. Something rammed into Jessie from behind. He slammed the butt of the rifle down on it.

"Come back to shore, Jessie. They're everywhere," Mike shouted.

Mike was right. The adrenaline that had kept him moving was fading. He was cold and his hands were shaking.

"Rory?" Where was he? Had he gone under again?

Then Jessie saw him, struggling to climb up onto the chopper. Rory slid as he was grabbed but he managed to kick free. Jessie started swimming the few meters between him and the chopper, determined to get Rory out of the water and away from the ichthyosaurs who thought he was dinner. Rory hauled himself up, blood streaming from his leg. Then he was up on the skids and out of the water.

Something nudged Jessie from underneath, but nothing bit him. Not yet anyway. Mike screamed from the shore, but

Jessie couldn't look back. He'd committed to helping Rory and he wasn't going to turn around. Mike was safe on the shore. All they had to do now was wait. He found a foot hold and dragged himself out of the water. Rory reached a hand down and then they were both perched on the upturned chopper.

The water wasn't that deep. He could've waded through the chest-deep lake, but swimming had been faster. He waved at Mike to let him know they were fine. When the water calmed down, they should be able to make it across. Behind him, the *Kronosaurus* arched and flopped as though trying to get back to deep water on the other side of the tear. Ichthyosaurs were close to it, maybe nibbling the bigger dinosaur.

Jessie exhaled and willed his heartbeat to calm. The last thing he needed was a heart attack. "You okay?"

"Mostly. Got bit."

"I'd offer to bandage it up, but I've only got the one I'm wearing." He forced a smile. But blood was running freely from Rory's leg, staining his jeans dark. Too much for it to be a simple bite. "I'd better take a look."

"Yeah." Rory tugged up the torn-up leg of his jeans. It wasn't neat gashes like Jessie's wounds were. This was ripped-open skin, and missing chunks of muscle. "I know it's bad. I think the dino blood in the water must have brought them over. But I'm glad I didn't stay in the chopper."

Jessie nodded. Even strapped in, staying would've been fatal. The risk of drowning, being crushed, and then being thrown. Getting out had been the better option. He glanced back at the portal. Night glimmered through the tear that stretched across the lake. When night fell here, it would be invisible.

Unless the *Kronosaurus* could turn around or swim backward, it was stuck. And it was far closer than Jessie liked. Several million years too close. He undid his belt.

"This is a really bad time for you to be getting your clothes off," Rory joked, but his eyes were framed with tension.

Jessie put the belt around Rory's lower thigh. "I'm trying to slow the bleeding. We might be home, but we're still a long way from help and your people haven't shown up yet."

"What's happening?" Mike yelled. They were only ten meters away, but it might as well have been a mile.

"Rory got a little bitten. You hurt?"

"Nah." He gave them the thumbs up. "I'm fine. And I have my phone." He lifted his shirt to reveal a package duct-taped to his torso. "I didn't want to lose it if I lived, and I wanted to make sure it was with me if I died."

"Good thinking. But there's no signal out here."

"SOS only, Uncle Jess. I think this counts."

"I think you're right," Jessie said. But he doubted Mike would get a signal. Reception was patchy this far from the house.

"I activated the emergency beacon before I got out of the R22. Those extra couple of seconds..."

"At least people will know we're in trouble."

The ichthyosaurs circled the chopper for a bit then drifted away. Not far enough that Jessie would recommend Rory get down though. Not yet. They'd have to wait this out.

Mike ripped the tape off and pulled the phone out of the plastic bag, then he plugged it into the power pack and tried to make the call. He paced around with his phone up like he was trying to find a signal. Jessie put more faith in the beacon.

He put his hand over Rory's. Help was on its way. All they had to do was wait. The chopper rocked beneath them, settling into the dirt below...or was something trying to dislodge them?

"Did you want to try for the shore?" Above them, the sky was turning pink and gold. He wasn't sure he wanted to make the swim in the dark when it would be harder to see the ichthyosaurs.

Rory grimaced. "Not really. We can wait until help arrives."

Mike put his phone in his pocket and sat down. "I couldn't get a signal."

"It's okay. The beacon was activated. Help is coming," Jessie called.

"We can always walk home in the morning."

Rory wouldn't be walking anywhere. If help didn't arrive tonight, he'd probably be dead. They had to figure this out, and that meant getting on to dry land.

"Where are your people?"

"Probably driving over to your place," Rory said.

So if they went to the house first, they were hours away. "You need to elevate your leg." The chopper rocked again, and Jessie froze. "Are you sure you want to stay here?"

Rory leaned back and put his wounded leg up on the skid. "Yeah. I don't want to risk being dinner again. This way, we get a little time together." He lifted Jessie's hand to his lips.

The *Kronosaurus* writhed and sent a splash of water over them.

"It's a bit hard to relax with that less than twenty meters away."

Rory glanced over. "At least it's not going anywhere."

"Don't be jinxing us." Or they would be making the swim whether Rory wanted to or not. "Are you sure you don't want to be on dry land?"

"Yeah." He tugged Jessie toward him, so they could lie together and look up at the stars. "Just need a bottle of wine."

Jessie snorted. Aside from the splashing of the *Kronosaurus*, the night was familiar. The stars were in the right place and even the insects buzzing were small and annoying. But something prickled at the edge of his mind and he couldn't relax, even though he was enjoying Rory's loose embrace.

He sat up. "Don't go to sleep."

"I won't. I've got you to keep me up." There was a glimmer of a smile.

Jessie rolled his eyes and sat up, facing the shore and Mike. Mike was still sitting, legs outstretched. "What's the first thing you'll do when we get home?"

"Sell my pictures to the highest bidder."

Jessie laughed and shook his head; though he was sure plenty of people would be interested, the government would probably confiscate them.

Mike glanced at the area of land that was part prehistoric where it had bled through. "Where have all the cows gone? There was a herd of them this morning."

Jessie frowned. "They probably wandered off. It's what they do."

Mike stood, phone in his hand the way it had been most of the time, but he wasn't recording. He was using the torch function and his attention was on the shrubs and the trees that didn't belong. "Aside from cows, what else lives out here?"

"Possums, snakes, feral dogs..." Jessie's stomach turned leaden. He could now add dinosaurs to that list.

Mike backed away from the plants and toward the water. "The dead cow this morning...it didn't die of natural causes, did it?"

"No..." but now it made sense. It looked like it had been picked clean, by crows or by dinosaur scavengers? But whatever had killed it had been bigger. Jessie picked up the rifle. "Get in the water and come to me."

Something moved, a fast, dark shape in the deepening shadows. Then it was running full tilt at Mike. Mike ran for the water, but he wasn't quick enough. The emu-dino slammed into him and took hold of his arm, shaking him like a rag doll and dragging him away. Mike screamed and used his phone to punch the creature in the face. The creature was just as determined not to let go.

Jessie couldn't shoot the dino without risking hitting Mike. He fired over their heads. The crack of the shot echoed through the night. It was enough for Mike to get a solid strike to the creature's eye. It released him and edged away, but clearly wasn't done as it danced around, waiting for another opportunity.

Jessie lined it up in his sights and fired. The emu-dino stopped, then crumpled. "Where's its partner?"

Mike cradled his arm next to his body. Even in the twilight, Jessie could see the spreading blood-dark stain. "I don't know, but it won't be far away."

CHAPTER 12

Jessie stared across the water. He couldn't see shit in the dark blue depths. Had the ichthyosaurs fucked off for the night or were they waiting?

He couldn't leave Mike there alone and bleeding. "Lie down."

"No, what if the other one comes?" Mike turned in circles as though expecting it to come running out of the darkness from any angle.

"Lie down so you lose less blood." If he'd been over there, then Mike wouldn't have been injured. He could've shot the thing before it attacked. He shouldn't have chosen to help Rory.

"Give me the rifle. I'll spot you." Rory put his hand out.

Around the helicopter, the water was dark and could be filled with waiting ichthyosaurs. He'd always thought his biggest problem on the land was feral dogs and snakes. He wished it still was. If he swam over and left Rory with the rifle, then he'd have nothing to fight the emu-dino with. But Rory was in a better place to make the shots because he was elevated.

"Don't pass out." Jessie handed over the rifle.

"I'll try not to." But the bleeding had slowed, and Rory seemed alert. The bigger danger now was if the tourniquet was too tight and he lost circulation to his leg. If help didn't come soon, Rory could lose the leg.

Jessie hesitated for a moment, before leaning in to kiss him. Rory pulled him close. "Go, before I change my mind about letting you feed yourself to the dinosaurs." He gripped the back of Jessie's neck and kissed him again. "Don't get eaten."

"I'll try not to."

"Okay. Go." Rory gave him a little push.

Jessie eyed the water. He hated swimming in the ocean. This just reinforced the fear that there was something lurking, waiting to eat him.

"Dive long and shallow, then swim as far as you can. It's quicker than wading," Rory added. Jessie wished Rory was coming with him, busted leg or not; they should be doing this together.

Jessie nodded. He knew that in theory swimming was faster, but his brain didn't like leaving his legs behind him for anything to eat.

Mike was still walking around, looking like wounded dinner. Did he not realize how hurt he was?

"If anything comes near you, I'll shoot it." Rory checked how many bullets were left in the rifle. "I'm ready."

Jessie wasn't. But he needed to move. He couldn't push off the helicopter too hard in case it moved and sent Rory tumbling into the water. And he didn't like diving too much either. If it were up to him, he'd climb down the side and then start swimming.

He was wasting precious seconds.

"Fuck." Then he dove, hoping to get as far away from the chopper as he could and as close to shore as possible. He surfaced and swam, thrashing and splashing until his knees hit the ground and he stumbled on to the shore. He glanced over his shoulder at Rory, still safe on the belly of the chopper, rifle at the ready.

Jessie ran over to Mike and hugged him. "Hey. Mike. Look at me."

It took a moment for Mike to focus. "You're here. I thought you'd left me."

"Nah, kid. I've got you." Jessie's hand was slippery with blood. It was pouring out of Mike. He dragged his nephew to the ground, knowing that the damage was more than he could fix with what he had to hand. "Just have a rest for a moment so I can check out the bite."

"Is the other one dead? There's always two, isn't there?"

"Yeah. Always two." He felt up Mike's arm, trying to find where all the blood was coming from. The arm hung loose like it had been torn from its socket. Had an artery been ripped up high? There was too much blood. "Hey, where's your phone? I could use the torch."

"I think I dropped it."

Shit. "I'll just have a quick look, okay? I won't be long." Jessie stood.

There was almost no light and he didn't want to leave Mike alone for more than a few seconds. He knelt back down and stripped off his T-shirt, then used it to wrap up Mike's arm tight. He didn't know if it would work, but there was nothing else he could do.

"How is he?" Rory called.

Losing blood, dying. He didn't want to say that out loud. "Fine. It's just a little bite. Shoulder looks dislocated."

Rory read between the lines and cursed softly. Even though Jessie couldn't make out the exact words, he felt the desperation in his soul. Rory knew they were screwed. If help didn't arrive soon, they'd be out of blood before they ran out of bullets.

"It's cold. Do you have a blanket?" Mike mumbled.

Jessie frowned and looked at his nephew. Mike was going into shock. "I'll have a look."

He got up and started walking slow circles around Mike, widening each time hoping that he'd find the phone. The body of the fallen emu-dino got closer with each turn. Then he saw a glimmer of light from the phone's torch, near the beast's tail. While he was sure the dino was dead, he didn't want to get that close.

With his foot, he hooked the phone away from the dino then picked it up. The screen flicked to life. It was a picture of Rosie in a sun hat. He'd told Mike off the first day he was here for treating her like she was a house pet and acting like he was seven, not seventeen. His throat thickened. He'd give anything to go back and not be such a grumpy shit. To make Rosie and Mike both feel more loved and wanted. To give Rory a chance instead of ducking and weaving like his life depended on being single.

The screen dimmed. Thirty percent battery. He turned off the torch.

He made his way back to Mike. "How's it going, kid? Help is on the way." He leaned over and embraced him. Mike's good hand fluttered against him. "I love you, Mike."

Jessie wasn't sure he'd ever told his nephew that before. He should've.

He sat back. All he could do was wait.

He wished he had some flares to lay out, but they were in the upturned R22 or maybe spread over the bottom of the lake. With nothing to do, he sat and held Mike's hand and stared over the water at Rory. He'd spent too much of his life waiting instead of living.

But that didn't stop him from listening for any noise that didn't belong. He wasn't sure if he was listening for dinosaurs or the beat of a rescue helicopter. Maybe both, with a mix of dread and hope churning in his gut.

Mike's grip went limp. Jessie searched for a pulse and found a faint one. Where was help? What was taking them so long?

Rory was resting on the skid, his vigil forgotten. Jessie peered into the shadows, expecting each one to move. At first, he thought it was his pulse he was hearing in his ears, but it was the steady thrum of the rescue helicopter.

He stood up.

The search light swept over the paddock. Jessie ran the couple of meters to meet it and stand in the blinding white light. He waved his arms. Stripped to the waist and covered in blood, he must look like a mad man.

He never saw the beast that crashed into him, knocking him to the ground.

CHAPTER 13

Jessie gasped for breath as the emu-dino grabbed at him. Its jaws snapped at his face. He rolled away from the dagger-like claws and got onto his belly, then his hands and knees, hoping to get up and run, but its claws raked down his back and got hooked on his jeans. Fabric tore, and hot blood washed over his skin as he tried to get free of the creature.

The helicopter kicked up dust and dirt, making it hard to see, and his eyes streamed.

He twisted, lashing out with his booted foot. The dinosaur grabbed his calf. Its claws sunk deep into his muscle and he screamed and fell. Then it was dragging him by the boot toward the ferns and away from the light.

The light tracked him.

Jessie swung his other foot at the dino's delicate shin and knocked it over. The dino didn't let him go; its claws ripped through his leg, but he was free. He scrambled away, limping toward the helicopter that was hovering, not landing.

What the fuck were they doing? "Help us!"

A medic leaned out the door. "What the hell is that thing?"

"A dinosaur. I can explain later." He hobbled as fast as he could toward the open door. Wanting to get off the ground even if that meant hugging a skid.

The dino was getting up. He wasn't going to reach the chopper in time.

Then the dino turned and ran toward the shore. Toward Mike.

"No." Jessie turned to go after it, knowing that he'd be too late.

The rifle barked twice.

The emu-dino went down and stayed down.

The pulse of air in his ears from the chopper blades was almost too much. He stumbled away from the reluctant medics, hot blood filled his boot, but he made it to Mike and started searching for a pulse.

Flood lights lit up the lake shore, the water and the R22 wreck, and further out the *Kronosaurus*. Everything was stark white and dark shadows and red blood.

Someone nudged him out of the way, so they could help Mike, and Jessie fell on his ass unable to get up.

Were all the emu-dinos gone? Or was there more lurking in the shrubs? What about the lake?

"Where are you hurt?" A woman peered at him.

Everything hurt. But that wasn't the answer she wanted. Where was he hurt the worst? He didn't know. "My back and my leg." But the injuries weren't going to kill him, not anytime soon anyway. "You need to get Rory." He pointed at him, still waiting on the upturned R22.

"What's in the lake?"

"Dinosaurs."

"Uh-huh," she said, like he had a head injury. "Have you been drinking? Using drugs?"

"Look at the bodies." He flung his arm out in the direction of one of the emu-dinos. "I run a cattle station. Do they look like cows to you?"

"Calm down."

How could he be calm? Was she not looking? He drew in a breath. She wasn't looking at the dinosaurs. She was too busy ruining his jeans to look at his leg. Jessie took a slow breath. "Is Mike alive?"

"Who's Mike?"

"The kid, over there," Mike was being loaded onto a stretcher. Were they being careful or rough? "My nephew."

"I don't know." She took his boot off. "I want to get you into the helicopter if you're going to cooperate."

Jessie stared at her. He was cooperating, but everyone he cared about had been eaten by dinosaurs and she wasn't paying attention. He swallowed down the anger that threatened to bubble up. "And Rory?"

She paused and looked around, as if really seeing for the first time. "Is he injured?"

"I put a tourniquet on his leg."

She stared at him. "What happened here?"

He considered telling her the truth again, but just shrugged. "I don't know. I just want to leave."

It was only after the medics had winched Rory up into the rescue chopper that Jessie let himself relax. A doctor fussed over Rory and Jessie looked away from the chewed-up mess of Rory's leg. Mike's face was uncovered, and they'd stuck a drip in him so that meant he was alive.

The helicopter's search light made a sweep of the lake and then lingered on the beached *Kronosaurus*. It was still alive, even if it wasn't going anywhere. Jessie was sure he should contact someone about the tear in time and the dinosaurs, but he didn't know who. And for the moment, it didn't matter.

All he wanted was a chance at living. He glanced at Rory. Really living.

EPILOGUE

Jessie stared at the hole in the ground, not listening to the priest drone on. Nothing he said would change anything. The suit hid the stitches and scars, but that was all that was holding him together.

Mike's footage had been sold and played ad nauseum. Until the next tear had appeared and a whole town had vanished. Gone in a blink.

Everyone was waiting for the next tear, with scientists busy trying to predict where so they could be ready. They had a theory for the why; something to do with the magnetic poles switching.

Other scientists were now trying to invent time travel using magnetic shifts.

Why anyone would want to go back deliberately, Jessie didn't know. Humans and dinosaurs shouldn't exist at the same time.

His property was crawling with scientists who didn't seem to care that he had a herd to muster and get to market. Another week they reckoned before he'd be free to go home and do anything. He wasn't even sure he wanted to go home.

Jessie scratched at the bandage on his arm. Now that the stitches were out, the healing wounds were itchy. His calf was much the same. At least he had a calf, and an arm.

A life.

He worked his jaw. It still ached from where his drunk brother had taken a swing and Jessie had let him. Steve wasn't lying. He had chosen Rory over Mike. He'd left his seventeen-year-old nephew alone on the shore, thinking he was safe. He should've known. He should've remembered the cow carcass and realized it was dinosaurs that had ripped it apart.

But everything about that night was a jumble of fear and pain.

He startled awake every night, thinking that thing was about to leap on him and rip his chest open. Then he'd pace around the hotel room until daylight so he could get a few hours' sleep before hospital visiting hours opened.

Jessie closed his eyes.

Two funerals in two days. There'd been no body to bury for Baz.

Mike hadn't survived the flight.

The back of Rory's hand brushed his and Jessie ignored the touch, needing to be alone with the grief for a little longer.

If it weren't for the people watching his every move, guarding him they said—more like protecting the reporters constantly shoving their cameras and microphones in his face. He opened his eyes. Black suited men stood around, and beyond them were the reporters looking for an angle. A new story to tell about the men who'd died and those who'd survived.

Dirt to dig.

Mike had been brave and caring. Things Steve had never seen in him. He should've punched his brother back and told him some truths. He was too much like their father, accepting only a narrow ideal of success and what a man should be. Jessie would rather be like Mike than either of them. If Mike were alive, he wouldn't be wasting a moment.

Jessie lifted his face to the clear blue sky; he had some living to do.

Then he moved his hand to clasp Rory's, not caring who saw their entwined fingers. Or what they thought, or what they said. Let them ask their questions.

The past had changed his future, and he wasn't going back.

THE END

 SEVERED**PRESS**

f facebook.com/severedpress
twitter.com/severedpress

CHECK OUT OTHER GREAT DEEP SEA THRILLERS

MEGA
by Jake Bible

There is something in the deep. Something large. Something hungry. Something prehistoric.
And Team Grendel must find it, fight it, and kill it.
Kinsey Thorne, the first female US Navy SEAL candidate has hit rock bottom. Having washed out of the Navy, she turned to every drink and drug she could get her hands on. Until her father and cousins, all ex-Navy SEALS themselves, offer her a way back into the life: as part of a private, elite combat Team being put together to find and hunt down an impossible monster in the Indian Ocean. Kinsey has a second chance, but can she live through it?

THE BLACK
by Paul E Cooley

Under 30,000 feet of water, the exploration rig Leaguer has discovered an oil field larger than Saudi Arabia, with oil so sweet and pure, nations would go to war for the rights to it. But as the team starts drilling exploration well after exploration well in their race to claim the sweet crude, a deep rumbling beneath the ocean floor shakes them all to their core. Something has been living in the oil and it's about to give birth to the greatest threat humanity has ever seen.

"The Black" is a techno/horror-thriller that puts the horror and action of movies such as Leviathan and The Thing right into readers' hands. Ocean exploration will never be the same."

CHECK OUT OTHER GREAT DEEP SEA THRILLERS

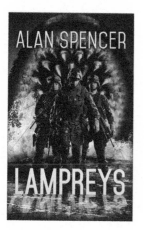

LAMPREYS
by Alan Spencer

A secret government tactical team is sent to perform a clean sweep of a private research installation. Horrible atrocities lurk within the abandoned corridors. Mutated sea creatures with insane killing abilities are waiting to suck the blood and meat from their prey.

Unemployed college professor Conrad Garfield is forced to assist and is soon separated from the team. Alone and afraid, Conrad must use his wits to battle mutated lampreys, infected scientists and go head-to-head with the biggest monstrosity of all.

Can Conrad survive, or will the deadly monsters suck the very life from his body?

DEEP DEVOTION
by M.C. Norris

Rising from the depths, a mind-bending monster unleashes a wave of terror across the American heartland. Kate Browning, a Kansas City EMT confronts her paralyzing fear of water when she traces the source of a deadly parasitic affliction to the Gulf of Mexico. Cooperating with a marine biologist, she travels to Florida in an effort to save the life of one very special patient, but the source of the epidemic happens to be the nest of a terrifying monster, one that last rose from the depths to annihilate the lost continent of Atlantis.

Leviathan, destroyer, devoted lifemate and parent, the abomination is not going to take the extermination of its brood well.

CHECK OUT OTHER GREAT
DEEP SEA THRILLERS

PREDATOR X
by C.J Waller

When deep level oil fracking uncovers a vast subterranean sea, a crack team of cavers and scientists are sent down to investigate. Upon their arrival, they disappear without a trace. A second team, including sedimentologist Dr Megan Stoker, are ordered to seek out Alpha Team and report back their findings. But Alpha team are nowhere to be found – instead, they are faced with something unexpected in the depths. Something ancient. Something huge. Something dangerous. Predator X

DEAD BAIT
by Tim Curran

A husband hell-bent on revenge hunts a Wereshark...A Russian mail order bride with a fishy secret...Crabs with a collective consciousness...A vampire who transforms into a Candiru...Zombie piranha...Bait that will have you crawling out of your skin and more. Drawing on horror, humor with a helping of dark fantasy and a touch of deviance, these 19 contemporary stories pay homage to the monsters that lurk in the murky waters of our imaginations. If you thought it was safe to go back in the water...Think Again!

Made in the USA
Monee, IL
10 July 2021